MATTEO

THE CONTI CRIME FAMILY
BOOK 4

C.M. STEELE

The Steele Press

INTRODUCTION

Matteo

My first kill was for her.

From that day on, I knew I'd always protect my dangerous little viper. However, I didn't understand how violently those protective instincts would change the day she turned sixteen. From then on, I protected not only her, but our future. Vivian belonged to me, and no one else. If you touched her, you'd pay.

I killed for her again, but it was one of my own this time.

And today, I crossed a line that solidified our fate and forced my hand, or so I made her believe. Sometimes you have to subdue beautiful but deadly creatures.

Vivian

How can you love and hate the same man in the same breath? He's powerful, handsome, dangerous, and evil—everything women in our world crave. When I was young, I wanted to be just like him. Then, as I grew, I wanted to be just with him, but I'm not that girl.

He sees me as underhanded, a menace, and a venomous animal. Not his future. Unfortunately, I forced his hand, intertwining our fates.

And to save face and to protect us, he's doing the unthinkable—making me his wife.

I have to get away.

PROLOGUE

MATTEO

"Don't fucking speak." She opens her mouth, letting out the slightest curse, and my hand pinches her mouth shut. "I said shut the fuck up, Viper." What was she thinking? My chest pounds out of control.

My pulse doubled the second I felt her presence in the area. It's normal when she's around. There's this feeling that's grown over the past few months. Shifted is more like it. After all, I've known Vivian her entire life. Still, the sight of her here sends my body into adrenaline overload.

It's my fault for not keeping a better eye on her, and it won't happen again. For all that Enrico is—our enforcer and much more—he sure as fuck dropped the ball when it came to his psycho princess. From the day she was born, they knew she was trouble, and since then, she hasn't stopped being a menace. Sixteen years, and Vivian has only gotten smarter, slyer, tougher, and more enchanting.

"Stay close, and don't move out of my protection," I warn her.

She pins me with a deadly glare, but I'm not intimidated. This is no place for her to be tonight. We're in the middle of a mob war with the Moreno Family. They want our area and are killing our people, stealing our shipments, and boldly threatening to kill our loved ones. We have no choice but to go bold.

Having Vivian here is the worst thing for us. If they get a hold of her, she could be used against us. Or worse, if something happens to her, I'll show no mercy on every Moreno.

With my eyes locked on hers, I growl out, "Are you listening?" Her throat muscles move and her pulse increases before she finally gives me the slightest nod. I want to release her and replace my hand with my mouth, but that's too damn wrong. Neither of us are ready for those repercussions.

"Vivian," Enrico hisses behind me so low we can just hear him.

I released my hand from over her mouth, hoping she doesn't go off the handle, but with her dad here to tame her ass, maybe she'll behave for a minute and understand the consequences. "She fucking followed you," I say through clenched teeth.

"Stay close to Matteo. Both of you need to be safe. You're the next generation," he reminds us. Damn right we are and one day we'll be creating his grandbabies, so I need her safe and sound while trying to keep my head in the game so I can stay alive long enough to create that family.

"Daddy, you need to be careful," she pleads, her voice so tender and sweet. Something about it touches me in a way I hadn't expected.

Fuck me; her worry hits me square in the chest, and that's why she can't be here. All of us will be worried about protecting her. Still, now isn't the time to get sentimental. It's time to get deadly.

We break off into groups. I keep Vivian close, but as I move to take out a round of guys, she dips off in another direction. Gunfire erupts and I'm fucking losing it, unable to find Vivian anywhere. I've dropped nearly a dozen guys, and she's nowhere to be found. The next room is where there's a hailstorm of gunfire, so I duck behind and go around the back, and that's when I see the horror.

I run back to find her too-careless ass and see my father clutching his arm and my woman having put one in the back of a Moreno hitman. She's shaking with the gun in her hand. I'm almost to her when I see a fucker come out of the darkness behind her. I'm inches away with my gun out, and she freaks—like I'd ever harm her.

"I didn't shoot your dad," she squeals.

"Move," I bark out. The bastard slices his knife in the air, swiping her skin as I let a bullet rip through the chamber that enters his head. He falls back and I rush to Vivian, whose eyes flutter and face pales. She's going to start freaking out, so I cover her mouth and drag her to the side up against a stack of pallets where it's safe for the moment.

When I see that she's finally learned to be quiet, I pull my hand off her lips—soft, pouty lips that hate me with a new, profound disgust that she would love to tell me all about, but she knows I'm at my wit's end.

I pull off my long-sleeved shirt and wrap it over her shoulder. "You shouldn't have been here."

"If I hadn't..." I shake my head while pressing my shirt to her wound. Shit, it's about a three-inch gash that's about an eighth of an inch deep, but it's bleeding pretty heavily.

I slam my eyes shut and then let them fly open to stare at my pain in the ass. "Yes, I am well aware of your skills, Viper, but this is a war that's not meant for little girls trying to be big boys."

"I'm not a boy." That's obvious to me and it's painful. I'm more than well aware that the little terror has grown up into a gorgeous young lady. Fuck, I've noticed.

Right now, it would be wrong as fuck to show her how much I've noticed. A part of me is unable to take the actions I want because she's too young to teach a real lesson, but another part is ready to fucking hold her to me, knowing she's safe.

"Then stop trying to be one of us. You're going to get yourself killed, and that would destroy your parents." It would kill me and the world would bleed, but I can't tell her that. "If that asshole had gotten a hold of you, we would have had to make a deal to get you back."

"Why would you?" She lifts her chin, daring me to lie to her, but the truth is simple. I can keep the complicated part to myself.

"Your father might not be the head of the family, but he's right up there, Viper. You're a princess, even if you want to be a fucking warrior." I wipe her wound that's going to need stitches. "That's going to leave a scar."

"Well, that's okay, because it's not for you to look at anyway." She takes my shirt and presses it to the wound. I need a doctor to look at her before I lose my cool.

"One day, someone will…" I'm cut off by footsteps behind me. I whip around and see my father approaching, holding his arm that's been wrapped up. Santos, my best friend, follows two steps behind him. His head tilts sideways as he spots Vivian, and confusion and concern cross his face.

"Let's get out of here. I need a word with you both." I nod, tension radiating through every bone in my body. Today could have gone a lot worse, especially if something happened to my fucking little viper. "Santos, ride in the other vehicle."

"Yes, Boss." He nods. "Good luck," he says to me, but then he shakes his head as he gives another glance in Vivian's way. He's probably thinking the same thing we all are. She wasn't supposed to be here and the risk was insane.

We only had a handful of women working for us, but they weren't like Vivian and they didn't ever get in the action like this. They stayed near the house or guarded our women on their shopping trips.

We get in the vehicle with Philo in the driver's seat, and my father immediately sings the viper's praises as he sits on the other side of her. "Great shot, Vivian."

"Yes, we're grateful for that, but she shouldn't have been here in the first place," I snarl, glaring at her while she sneers at me through the darkness of the vehicle.

"Son." The warning is clear. I need to leave her alone before I go too far and say something that gets me in trouble. As the next in line, many would see my lack of concern for my father as my interest in overthrowing him. It's not like that at all. I love my parents completely and I'll take over when it's time and not a moment before.

"Sorry, Father, but as you can see, I'm sure this is only going to spur her on," I argue. I'm grateful he's alive, but Vivian's safety means the world to me. He's about to snap on me when the door opens.

"The hell it is. Young lady, you're not doing this shit again," Enrico barks, jumping into the front passenger seat. I swear I could see the new gray setting in his hair as he speaks. I'm glad I have someone on my side regarding this matter.

"Yes, Father," she replies so meekly and filled with contrition as she momentarily dips her head that I almost believe her, but then Viper lifts it up with a smirk. "Or I'll wait until I join another family before I engage in action."

I'm fucking grateful that the darkness of night keeps the shadow on me because the venom practically seeping from my mouth would be visible as I ask, "What's that supposed to mean?"

She looks at me and then turns away with an air of arrogance. "Matteo reminded me that I'm a mafia princess, and princesses find their mafia prince to marry. There are lots of bonds to make instead of wars." She cracks her knuckles, and I feel like I fucking stuck my foot in my mouth. She's not marrying another mafia prince. Over my fucking dead body.

Still, I'll fix that shit. There's only one prince for her, and when she's grown, she'll be my fucking queen.

PROLOGUE

VIVIAN

It's been two weeks since Matteo put a bullet in that guy's head, rescuing me from danger and protecting me—then breaking my heart with his next words. My hero and my enemy in one moment.

I look in the mirror, checking my wound for the dozenth time. It hasn't fully healed, but Matteo's right; there will be a nice scar in its place. A sigh falls from my lips as I stare at myself.

What's wrong with me? Sometimes I behave irrationally, especially when it comes to Matteo. *"She followed you here,"* he barked out to my father. But that wasn't the truth. I followed him. Slowly I've come to the realization that my interest in Matteo wasn't to be like him, but a desire to be with him.

"Matteo," I sigh. Tall, strong, and handsome. His dark eyes are always penetrating when he stares, even when he's looking to scold me. The brooding way he carries himself, the entire room always takes notice. The women surely pay attention to the heir, the underboss of the Conti Crime Family. Every man wants to be him and the women want to be with him. I've just become one of those ladies, and I think my heart's cracking.

There's a knock on my bedroom door. Gasping, I adjust my robe and wipe my eyes with my palms.

"Who is it?" I call out. My voice cracks, catching me by surprise. Clearing my throat, I repeat myself a little louder.

"It's me, Vee. Can I come in?" My brother's voice does me some good, but I'm not ready for him to see me like this.

"Give me two minutes." I slip on a tee shirt and shorts that I'd planned on wearing before I wasted time feeling sorry for myself.

Before I open the door, I steal one more look at myself in the mirror and, gratefully, there is no sign of my pain. When I open it, he's smiling at me with his arms wide open. "Gio, how are you?"

"I'm good. It's you I'm worried about. Pops just told me what happened. Damn, killer. You are one tough cookie, but you could have been killed." He squeezes me tighter, and I welcome it. Usually I'm not the hugging type, but frankly, I haven't been myself.

He's right. For the past two weeks, I've hardly left my room and the house because of the fear. Things with the Moreno Family have calmed down, but it's only a matter of time before things start up again. Maybe I'm not as tough as I thought I was. Or maybe it's my heart that has the bigger problem. I'm afraid of seeing Matteo again. It's only a matter of time before I do and then I'll have to face my new demons, learning how to act like a girl a man would want, especially a man like Matteo.

"Mom wants you to go to dinner with us," he says.

"Go to dinner? Where?"

"At the Conti Mansion." I mask my expression, but I want to fall out.

"Yeah, well. Maybe not tonight."

"I don't think you're going to get away with it that easily. I saw Aunt May over here earlier gushing about you coming tonight." Yes, I've already received a beautiful necklace from her as a thank you gift for saving her husband.

"I know. Thanks for the heads up. I might be in her good graces, but I'm on Matteo's shit list."

"That's because you're like a little sister to him and he's worried about you. Give it time. He's grateful that his father's alive too, and that wouldn't have happened if it wasn't for you, killer." He kisses my cheek and leaves. I think I'll fake sick tonight for sure.

CHAPTER ONE

MATTEO

TWO YEARS LATER

I POUND AWAY AT THE PUNCHING BAG, attempting to alleviate the violent tension in my shoulders. Each strike of the bag is supposed to take some of it away, but nothing seems to do the trick. Adrenaline courses down my body as I pummel the damn thing to death, sending the contents spilling out onto the wooden floor.

The racket echoes in the room, sending one of my men in to see if I need any assistance. "Are we going hunting today, boss?" Whenever I'm on edge, which is almost always caused by the same person, we go and terrorize some shit, but today isn't that day.

"No—just clean this up," I command, heading to grab another bag from the supply closet.

"Yes, Mr. Conti."

"Fuck. Calm down, killer," I grunt to myself, carrying the heavy bag to the hanging rack. Unhooking the ruined bag, I replace it with a new one and continue where I left off, this time removing my soaked shirt and wiping my face.

In just my boxers and sneakers, I throw punches left and right. My shoulders are starting to feel the effort, but my mind is still running wild. Sweat drips down my bare chest as I knock the bag harder than ever, reminding me of what now covers it. A smirk spreads over my face. She's going to love it.

Tonight has to be perfect because it is the night I'll claim and capture my little viper and set her up in her new home. There's a lot riding on the success of my mission. I've never wanted anything more than this, and I will succeed.

I've longed for her for years; well before I should have. Five years older than her, I've spent my life guarding my little devil queen. Then, one day, that protective familial bond broke and something else took its place: lust. I saw her and knew that no one, no female, could ever compare to my viper.

My first kill was for her. She'd been vulnerable under the little dangerous shell she walked around with. I hit the bag harder, remembering that day all over again.

He'd been watching her like a sick stalker, but he had no idea that the little mafia princess wasn't alone. She had a big family, a prince who would one day be king, and no one laid a hand on his subjects. Little Vivian was walking to class with her Draculaura bookbag, ready to bring hell to her third-grade class. Smart and sassy, she drew the attention of the sick fuck behind the desk.

After coming from classes, I saw his attention to her when no one was looking. Even Vivian wouldn't have noticed because it was sly, always when her attention was away from him. The light touches bothered her, but she didn't say a word. No, my little charge just moved away, dropped chalk in his coffee. It explained why she'd been caught packing a blade when going to school. She was aware but didn't tell anyone. We'll take out the trash for her.

I would make sure to watch closer, setting up cameras. Then one day, I called in a favor. By the end of the day, we had every bit of info from his computers and several photos he had hidden.

Enrico was ready to rip the man limb from limb, but I said, "This one is mine. Finders keepers." Enrico stared at me strangely before turning to my father, only for my father to shrug. I'm not sure what they were discussing, but I wanted Williams' head.

"I'll bring him to you tonight," he snarled.

My father, who is the only rational one at the present moment, intervenes while my uncle Alessio pours Enrico a drink. "Are you prepared for this, son? You're only thirteen."

"She's a part of this family and has no idea the real danger she's in."

"Okay, son. After all, this Family will be yours one day." We shake hands and part ways.

In the middle of the night, I have a middle-aged, balding fuck with a sack over his head, sitting in front of me. I pulled it off to see Enrico didn't take him quietly and managed to get in a few rounds. I can't blame him.

"Well, Mr. Williams. Can I call you Mr. Williams? What am I saying? It doesn't matter what you're called because you won't be alive much longer."

"What? I didn't do anything."

"No, that's where you're wrong. You are so wrong. See, you have committed an egregious offense that demands penance. You dared to violate a child. His child."

"I didn't touch her."

I backhand the fucker. "Now that's a lie." Enrico's being restrained by my father and Alessio. "Do you want to keep lying?"

"I only touched her in an appropriate manner."

"We all know that's a lie. I saw your hands on my Viper."

"You're lucky she didn't chop them off herself, but she's searched before she leaves for school. Now, we're not there anymore, and let's just say I'm not interested in your lies."

"I swear I didn't mean anything by it. She's just pretty." Enrico roars behind me and I know I don't have the time I want to torture the fucker.

Whipping out my hunting blade, I fist his hair and snapped his head back. "She's pretty, but you meant everything by it. We're done with your lies and you're not going to touch her again, right?"

"Yes, yes. I promise I won't."

"I know you won't." Swiftly, I slice it across his throat, sending arterial spray everywhere. Instead of fear, disgust, or panic, all that washes over me was pride. I protected my family.

Ten years later and I'd kill for her again and again. Protecting Vivian was my life goal, and she'd make sure it was a busy one. That brutally beautiful woman was getting more and more daring. Even though she wanted to act tough, all I saw was the sexiest thing alive.

Her dark-reddish curls bounce with attitude and her hazel eyes are filled with intent, and I want them focused on me as I take her, making her mine. The amount of fantasies I have made it hard to get shit done and have turned me into a big asshole, although it has made me an even darker mob boss than my father.

She is meant to rule at my side. She is everything I could want in a wife and more. Not to mention, she's fucking stolen my heart and I wasn't aware that was possible. Now to make it happen.

A barely legal woman, Vivian Barone is a terror to handle, like a baptized cat. I have my hands full. First things first —I have to speak with her father.

A knock on the door sends him in before I expect to see him.

"Matteo, it's good to see..." His words freeze in his mouth when he spots the tattoo on my chest. It's new, and the meaning is clear. Although it wasn't meant for his eyes, I'm not ashamed or bothered by it. One day soon, the right person will see it and understand.

Enrico's expression stiffens and then he says, "I suppose there's a specific reason you called me in here today." His eyes move right back to the tattoo.

"Yes, although I told my father I wanted to see you after my workout," I grunt.

He adjusts his suit cuffs. "Well, now is as good a time as any. My day is pretty full, as you're well aware."

"Yes, I suppose it is. We're family in more ways than one. I've looked to you for guidance, and although I've taken over for my father and I'm technically your boss, I'm coming to you as a man when I say that I want to marry your daughter."

He chuckles. Shaking his head, Enrico says, "Boy, Matteo, you do love a challenge, don't you? The family and my daughter all in the same week?" Yes, I've only just taken the reins this week, but I'm more than capable and if anything, I need my queen by my side to do it.

"I love Vivian."

"Well, if you can get her to marry you, I'm all for it. Just don't hurt my little girl. She's crazy enough to return the favor."

"I'm well aware of who she is. I happen to think she's the perfect woman to be at my side, and I'm sure you know that if anyone is capable of being the wife of a mob boss, it's Vivian."

"Shit, she'd rather be the boss."

"You might have a point there," I chuckle.

"So, when will you tell her? You haven't been secretly dating, have you?" He narrows his eyes at me.

"No, I haven't approached my little viper." She may be his daughter, but she's going to be my bride, and I won't debate that with anyone else. If anyone dared challenge me, we'd have a problem, but I can't blame him. If he knew about the thoughts I have about his baby, he'd use his skills on me.

"So a quick strike is what you're going for," he says, staring at me with a smirk. Enrico understands Vivian isn't the kind of woman to fall at my feet, so I'll have to demand her submission or show her how damn good she could be as my better half. Either way, she doesn't have a choice.

"If necessary."

"Good luck. I have to talk to security about the party tonight, but I will wait until you speak to her before I mention it to my wife." He scrunches up in fear because Vivian didn't get all that attitude from him.

"Good. I'll wait until the party is over. I don't want to ruin her special evening." A sense of ease comes from him, which is what I expected.

"You know I've invited men from two other families, right?"

"Yes," I growled. The thought of another one of the families with their sons vying for my woman's attention is unbearable, even for a second. "She's mine."

"Maybe you should have told me a little sooner."

"I'm not afraid of the others. In fact, I'll make it clear that she's taken by the end of the night." I'm not sure how I'll do it without declaring my sentiments, but it will be done. I think about the comments she made about marrying into another mafia family. When those words escaped her lips, I wanted to tell her then and there that it wasn't going to happen. Not ever. She belonged to me and nothing would change that fact.

"No killing. We don't want a war," my father says, walking into the room. It's been quiet for a long while, which is good. The Morenos went back to lick their wounds after our payback two years ago. I hadn't gotten enough revenge on them, but one day I would. They came after my family; first my father and then my future wife.

"Yes, Father," I say, nodding slightly, and then continue with a warning of my own. "But remember—if anyone puts a hand on Vivian, I'll chop it off." Just the thought of another man's hands on my girl will send me over the edge. People think I'm crazy deadly now, they have no damn idea how psychotic I can be. I won't just let the world burn, I'll tear it apart piece by piece first before setting it ablaze.

He frowns yet gives a relenting nod. "Understood, but we deal with it privately."

"You turned this over to me for a reason." If he didn't think I was prepared, he should have held onto the reins a tad bit longer. "Do you doubt my ability to run the family?"

"No, hell no, but I remember what it was like to be obsessed. We all do, and you'd do anything and everything for the woman who you can't live without." He has a point, but frankly, now isn't the time for a lecture. I have enough tension to fight a bull, and they aren't helping.

"Very well. If you two will excuse me, I have to shower and handle some matters before I prepare for the party." I take a towel and throw it around my shoulders, covering my chest.

I step around both men, ending the discussion. I respect both of them, but I am the head of the Conti Family now, and I will do as I please when it comes to my sweet viper. Anyone places a hand on my queen, and my wrath will be swift and deadly.

Leaving the gym, I head upstairs and into my bedroom where I can be left alone, so no one asks any more damn questions. Irritation grows. Knowing there are men looking to marry my queen, and that she might not have any objections, pisses me off. They'll want to touch and kiss her, and that shit isn't acceptable.

The only hands I want on her soft, dangerous flesh are mine.

Stripping out of my clothes, I turn on the shower and climb in. I groan as the hot water hits my chest and goes to my hard cock. Quickly, I'm gripping it, looking for relief, but I know the only thing that will bring me satisfaction is Vivian's sweet, lithe body in my hands.

Soon, she'll be under the spray with me, moaning while I'll scrub that little scar on her shoulder. That memory will be forever etched in my mind. She was nicked with a knife when she followed her father on an assignment and a fucker got out of pocket, but I ended that piece of dirt before he could do anymore damage.

Every time I see that scar, I itch to reach out and kiss it, lick it. With each encounter, it's getting harder and harder to resist the temptation.

She has been trouble from the day she was born, but I wouldn't have it any other way; I suspect that our brief engagement will be no different.

CHAPTER TWO

VIVIAN

IT'S MY EIGHTEENTH BIRTHDAY, AND MY PARENTS are planning on throwing me a party. It's a big one with a couple of men from different mafia families so that I can make an alliance. Personally, I don't have any interest in it, but what can you do? It's my fault for saying I was interested in meeting and making connections, so now they're making it happen. They always try to give me what I want even when I'm a big pain in the ass.

My biggest crush, Matteo Conti, will be there, and I'm sure he'll just scowl and stare like he does, giving me warning glances to behave. He has just been crowned the head of the Conti Family and doesn't see me like the other women in our world. How could he, when I've never acted like one?

We rarely run into each other unless it's when I'm up to no good. It's almost like he's keeping tabs on me to ensure I stay in my place. Given the family business, it was probably smart to keep me locked down, so I didn't get them into trouble. Still, to him, I can never behave, so maybe it's for the best that I meet with some of the other men from the families. They're cute and buff like Matteo. They don't have that energy that gives me chills and feelings in all my girly places, but I'm sure that will come with time.

AFTER GETTING DRESSED FOR THE DAY, I WENT downstairs for breakfast where my mom had set up a full buffet. My eyes shoot wide open at the massive feast. She made sausage, bacon, eggs, hash browns, and pancakes this morning as if we're all going to devour it. I understand my limits even after a long day of training. I can't eat a fraction of this food. "Mom, this is too much."

She tilts her head with a big smile, stepping around the counter to give me a hug. "It's your birthday, baby girl."

"Thanks," I say, kissing her cheek. For eighteen years, I've given her hell. If I ever have children, I'm sure I'll be having Satan's spawns, the devil's creations, for certain. The prospect of having a husband sounds scary now that I'm on the precipice.

"So, what are your plans? College?" We've hovered around the subject, but I've changed it often. My parents haven't really pressured me either way. When it came to school I was a mediocre student, smart but disobedient. Grades had never been an issue, but my temper and tolerance for jackass teachers and boys with raging hormones were. Although I did have a host of guards who made sure little perverts at school only bothered me once.

"Come on, Mom. Can you see me at some college? I'll probably get kicked out after a week or end up in prison for murder," I explained. My temper gets the better of me all the time and I don't need to add jail time for ripping off a guy's balls if he gets handsy.

She sighs, brushing a stray red curl behind her ear. "True. I suppose that's why your father has brought in several men for you to meet. Although there are many things you can still do."

"I don't know what I want to do." There's only one thing I want, but the possibility is nearly impossible. I want to rule by Matteo's side and let him touch me like a man does a woman that he can't resist.

"You can do anything you feel like. You're only eighteen. When I was your age, my parents tossed me out onto the street, leaving me to fend for myself. You can live here until you're old and gray. It's your choice, sweetie."

"Your parents were cunts," my dad says, coming through the door.

"That they were," I say. We've never met her parents and never will. They're still kicking, but we wouldn't know anything about them because they betrayed my mom a long time ago, and that will never be forgiven. I've heard that they're living on a very fixed income, and my dad might have something to do with it. I don't doubt it, since he'd do anything for my mother. I'm surprised they're living after what they did. My dad isn't known for his forgiveness to slights against his family.

"Happy birthday, little devil." He kisses the top of my head and then pulls me in for a bear hug. "You look adorable this morning. Are you excited about tonight?" he adds. I love my dad, even if he's being a bit extra right now.

"What's going on?" I asked him, eyeing him suspiciously. He seems way too cheerful.

He wraps his arms around my mother's waist. "Nothing. I can't say happy birthday to my baby?" She shoves a piece of bacon into his mouth, and I wonder if they're both working together on something they're not saying.

My eyes narrowed into slits as I read the room. "Yeah, but um…something seems different with you."

"Today's a big day," my father says, stealing a drink of my mother's orange juice.

I raise my brow and stare at him with mistrust. "Why—are you selling me to one of the guys tonight?" I'm sure he wouldn't, but that doesn't mean I can't ask.

He scoffs. "Come on… you know I couldn't sell you to any of them. You'd cut their balls off before the wedding night."

"You got that right." I snag a sausage link and bite off a big chunk while staring right at my father dead in the eyes and then smile.

He clutches his bits behind the counter while my mother pets his shoulder. "Ouch. The man that marries you will have hell to pay, but I'm sure you'll find someone who is your equal."

There's only one. My stomach flutters, then rolls as I think about him. It's like that all the time. A whirlwind of bodily functions rushing through my system nearly causing a scene whenever I think of the man. It's hard to stomach the idea of anyone being his but me, unfortunately it will happen one day.

"Probably not," I say, shrugging off his comment pretending to be unfazed. I prepare a plate, no longer feeling hungry when I consider that the only one who makes me feel that way is Matteo, and he's not interested. The last time we spoke, he was telling me to go home and called my father on me. Then he went to a party where there were tons of beautiful women. I'm sure he took one of them home.

Even though the food is delicious, I can't taste it because all I can think of is the pain in my chest. Most days I can ignore my feelings for Matteo, but today they'll be thrown into the spotlight since I'll be surrounded by several men, including him. Unless...he doesn't bother to show up. I hadn't even considered that idea until that horrible thought slashed through my brain.

Matteo is now the boss of the Conti Criminal Family and doesn't need to show up to the party for the daughter of one of his men. I've become more inconsequential to him in a matter of days. My heart can't handle not seeing him even though I ache when I do see the man.

"Thank you for the amazing breakfast." I put my plate in the dishwasher and kissed my mother's cheek. "I need to do some reading."

"Reading?" It's my father's turn to eye me with suspicion. Of course, almost everything I do is suspect because I'm messed up in the head, so he's right to be curious.

"Yeah. Research on the prospective men coming tonight," I answer without hesitation.

"Do you need a list?" my mother offers, smiling brightly. She pulls out her phone like she already has it prepared.

"No, but I'm guessing you invited every available Bianchi and their families as well as the Black family, even though they don't have mafia ties but only have sons." They are all super-hot men, and any girl would like to have them, but I'm not interested. Still, I should give it a chance because Matteo isn't interested in me.

"Yes, and don't forget the Conti Family boys." I'm so damn glad I'm a professional at masking my expressions, so they can't see the shitstorm going off inside my head right this second.

"Oh yeah. I didn't even consider them because they're not on the table. I'll be up in my room." I roll my eyes and head up, waving to them as I disappear, heart pounding with each step.

As I open my bedroom door, I find a card and a rose on my bed. Someone was being sneaky. I wonder if my father put it in there and that's why he was acting weird.

I ran my hand across the beautiful script. *Happy Birthday, Viper.*

Gasping, the words inside change my mood completely, setting plans in motion.

Everything changes today. Wow, I can't believe what I'm reading, so I read it again and smile. *Time to act.*

CHAPTER THREE

MATTEO

"MY LITTLE VIPER, WHAT ARE YOU DOING NOW?" I growl, adjusting my cock as I watch the monitors from my bedroom computer. I tracked her signal until she showed up on the cameras outside the mansion near a large group of trees.

Fuck. She's in a sexy little number as she sneaks across my property. It's cute that she believes I can't see her as if this place hasn't been fully secured. It's her eighteenth birthday, and the mischievous brat must be up to something.

Ever since that time at the warehouse I've kept better track of her, but that doesn't mean she doesn't give me a run for my money. It's almost as if she tries to test me, and she most certainly has over the past decade. Sometimes it was fun, but others I hated being the bad guy. She was always getting pissed at me when I caught her sneaking out of school. As long as she wasn't meeting some boy, it didn't bother me that much. Hell, I didn't know a woman smarter that her, so she could ditch the bullshit, but she still needed someone to look after her and her guards couldn't keep up.

School in itself was a problem. I wish her little ass was homeschooled, but then that would have never flown with her because she wouldn't have liked being caged in and rebelled there too. The number of shitheads I had a talking to or put in the hospital decreased over the years, but there was always a tough or new guy who saw me or Vivian as a challenge he had to conquer. The motherfucker would fuck around and find out that I wasn't that guy.

Twice I had to clean up after her mess because she shanked them and let's just say weapons aren't allowed on school property. Still, the assholes deserved it because no one puts their hands on her, but I got them to shut their fucking mouths. The day she graduated, I was grateful to get her away from all the young fuckers, and even watched from a security camera nearby.

The woman doesn't know how much of her life I've been a part of and for the time being I have no intention of telling her or I might end up the one shanked. She's crazy like that, and I'm a sucker for her brand of nuts.

I fix my all-black suit, tucking my gun in its holster, ready for trouble at any time of day even though I have plenty of security.

Since I woke up, there has been this nagging sense of tension, and I'm not quite sure it's just getting Vivian in my arms. Maybe it's my new position, but a new paranoia is sinking in that wasn't there previously.

Stealing one more look at my woman's movements, I'm caught off guard and intrigued. Then again, that's nothing new when it comes to her.

"What are you playing at?" I whisper, staring at the feed. With a last-minute look at my appearance, I adjust my collar and then leave my bedroom. Quickly and quietly I head down to my office where she just disappeared into. My guards are patrolling the house, but if they see her, they won't say a word because she's my best enforcer's daughter.

Hell, he was my father's best enforcer, and even though he's the oldest man working for us, he kills better than all the other men I have. My father and Enrico taught me everything I know about enforcing our will. Now, I'm about to teach his little girl a lesson that's going to last a lifetime. She will always be mine.

Quietly, I use the secret entrance, so she doesn't know I'm there, but then I'm stunned.

I walked into a sight that sends me over the edge. Never once have I been out of control, but this has done it. Everything I do is calculated, methodical, planned because it's vital to the organization and my family.

Vivian knows just how to push me to react, and boy, do I ever. Santos, my second-in-command, has one hand around her throat and his other hand on her fucking pussy, leaning her over my desk with most of his body pinning her down.

"I don't give a fuck whose daughter you are. You need to be fucked and taught a lesson. You don't play with the big boys." Hearing the words out of his mouth, knowing those words I have said in my head a million times when it comes to her, only adds to my ire. She's mine, and he has touched her.

For all of Vivian's toughness, she can't fight his strength. Tears rim her eyes, and I can see the actual fear in them. I read the situation wrong, which only doubles my rage. They weren't meeting for a tryst. He was attacking my future wife.

He isn't a little guy, and now she's put herself in a situation where without my help, she's screwed. Son of a bitch. Nothing but his death will be suitable.

"Do you mind telling me what the fuck is going on?" I say, sending two sets of eyes my way, only one pair I give a fuck about. Eyes that I never want to see like that again. It's the fucking first time in my life that I understand the depth of my obsession. He jumps back, releasing his filthy hands from her fragile neck and hot pussy.

"Oh, boss. We were just having a discussion." Every word out of his mouth only makes it worse. My teeth grind together, nearly cracking with the weight of my jaw clenching. He's clearly lying straight to my face, but what else is there to do. After all, he knew my intentions for her and above all else, she's our enforcer's daughter.

"A discussion? Is that true, Viper?" She looks at him and then back at me, trying to decide what her play will be. I don't waste time. My gun is out and aimed. I shoot him right there, sending him to the floor.

Walking up to her, I fist her hair, tugging her head back. "You were about to lie to me. You know I hate it, and yet you persist."

"Why did you do that? Jealous?" she tosses back like what just happened—didn't.

Several of my men bust through the door with their guns out, ready to deal with a threat. "Relax, men. Clean up the mess, and remember that this is what happens when you betray me. Excuse us." I drag her from the room and take her upstairs to my bedroom where I plan to teach her a fucking lesson. She might be playing that shit cool, but it's not the truth in her eyes at all. He was seconds from taking what she wasn't offering, but he wanted to lie to me.

She doesn't put up a fight. I don't know if it's because she's still shaken up from him, or she's smart enough not to fucking test me at the moment.

As soon as I close the bedroom door, she turns to me and says, "What are we doing in your bedroom?"

"You know this is my bedroom?" I challenge. She's never been inside here. No woman has, no matter how many times I pictured her naked body on my sheets sweating them up with that hint of floral scent that lies on her pale skin.

"Come on, Matteo. You've lived in this home all your life. Your parents only moved out of the main house last week when you became the Don." She rolls her eyes at me. I swat her fucking ass.

She gasps and stares at me with that smart mouth open, wide enough to stick the tip of my dick inside. "Don't fucking roll your eyes at me. I'm not in the mood for your shit today, Viper."

She moves close, nearly pressing her ample chest against mine, daring me. "Then let me go home." I tug off my tie and stare into her bright, beautiful eyes. They're hazel, mostly green with flecks of brown.

"Not yet. We need to talk." I wrap my fingers around a few loose strands of her dark, reddish-brown curls, gliding my hand through the smooth texture with many thoughts in my head.

"We don't have anything to say to each other." Her eyelashes flutter and her pupils dilate, telling me more than her mouth could ever say. She might have been scared of Santos, but fear's not what is happening now. My girl wants what I do.

Growling, I cuff her small hands in mine and turn her around, wrapping my tie tightly in place on her wrists. "What the fuck, Matteo? Let me go."

"Do you know who you're talking to, fucking little girl? Like you said, I'm the Don, and I said we need to talk."

Dragging her over to my bed, I flip her onto her stomach, pinning her onto my lap and staring at her skirt. Since when does the viper wear a skirt? She looks so damn delectable that my dick is hard as steel, ready to impale this sexy imp on it. "You made me kill one of my top men, Viper. Don't tell me that you wanted that asshole just to piss me off some more, because it won't work."

"What are you doing?" she asks, twisting her head to look up at me with those pretty eyes that have had me aching for that little pussy for way too long.

"What you've needed to be done. Something your parents should have done a long motherfucking time ago." My hand comes down on her skirt-covered left ass cheek.

She yelps and then calls me an asshole. "Stop."

"No." I go for the next one. "Look what you made me do. My men are now wondering if they're next. I killed one of my top capos, my best friend. Do you get that? You forced me to put a bullet in my best friend's head."

"Couldn't have been that good of a friend." She's right about that, but that damn attitude makes me want to drill her tight pussy to the bed and keep her coming all night long.

"Fucking hell. I'm always cleaning up after you, Viper. It's like you want me wrapped up in your mess. Now, you're going to pay. What the fuck were you doing in my office in the first place?"

"None of your business." The fucking audacity of her never ceases to amaze me. No one would speak to me like that, but Vivian has never been right in the head. Pushing my buttons seems to be her goal, and I must be fucked up too because I eat it up like candy.

"See, that's the shit that gets your ass spanked." This time, I need to go further. I lift up her fucking short skirt and find her in a pair of black panties. Shaking my head, I tug them down violently. I'd rip them off, but there is no way I'd let her walk out of here with her pussy bare in front of my men. The risk of anyone seeing what belongs to me is too fucking much. I've already had another man's hands on what belongs to me.

"What the hell?" she gasps, trying to scramble off me, but I grip her by the throat like a snake to stop it from striking.

"Don't move, or I'll make this so much fucking worse, Viper. What were you doing in my office?"

"Nothing." Still, she refuses to concede.

"Do you live here, Viper?" I ask, knowing that soon she will.

"Nope," she answers with a sassy pop of the "p" sound.

I grip her ass cheek firmly before slapping it. "Then what the fuck were you doing in my office?"

"Why do you call me Viper?" she asks instead of answering my damn question. This woman is pure frustration, but I'll give her a taste of what she wants since she's taking her punishment so well.

Tilting her head so I can look into those gorgeous eyes, I say, "Because you sneak around, and you bite when you sense danger. Now, answer me." She doesn't say a word, so my hand comes down on her ass.

The sound of my hand coming off her supple flesh is music to my ears. It almost makes me forget the fucked-up sight I had before me. "Why was my capo so close to you, touching you?"

"I don't know." Her voice is soft and meek; nothing like the damn Viper I know..

"Don't lie to me. I heard what he said to you. He wanted to fuck your virgin pussy."

She whips her head at me with such ferocity. "Who the hell says I'm a virgin?"

Man, she's asking for it. I press my finger in her hole and can't get past the second knuckle, even though her cunt is soaked with need. "I know you are. You're a lot of things, but loose isn't one of them, and you've never been on a date, Viper."

"You don't know everything about me."

"I don't, but I know enough to know you need to learn a real lesson." I continue to pop her little ass, watching it turn red and her pussy get wetter. Her lips part, eyes closing.

"Fuck, you're making a mess on my pants."

She tilts her head and glares at me. "And that's my fault too?"

"No. You can pretend to hate me all you want, but your body doesn't lie like your mouth does."

"I do hate you. It's called adrenaline. Is my punishment over?" That sass is a fucking front. My girl isn't as tough as she wants to play with me, but she doesn't know she's my only weakness. She doesn't know I'd kill all my men for her.

"It's only getting started." I massage her massive, reddened globes, parting them to look at her soaked cunt and that little puckered hole. Fuck, I could nut right this second just thinking about my plans. They've changed, and Vivian has given me my opening. One I'm going to take, and the party be damned. I'm not going to wait that long.

I slide her onto me, straddling my legs and holding her hands behind her back while she glares at me. "I hate you, Matteo."

"Don't tell lies, Viper." She spits in my face, but that doesn't do her good.

I crush my mouth to hers, sliding my fingers between her legs. She moans, opening her pretty lips, and I slide my tongue inside. She attempts to bite me, but I bite her lip. "Don't be mean, or I won't let you come, beautiful."

"Matteo," she gasps.

"Yes, Amore."

"I hate you."

"Mean it, and maybe I'll believe it." She cries out on my fingers, shaking as her tight little pussy comes on my digits. I pull my hand from between us and bring it to my lips, sucking off her release. "So fucking good."

Her eyes heat and her lips part, but she's too stunned to speak. "Now it's time to finish what I started." I lift her off me and toss her onto her belly. She bounces so sexily on my bed, tied up with her hands behind her back. Fuck me—I love having my viper at my mercy, especially when she comes so easily for me.

"What are you doing?" The sound of my zipper grabs her attention. "You're going to fuck me like this?" She sounds hurt. I wouldn't take her virginity so callously.

"Not yet."

I open my pants, free my cock, and then adjust her so her knees are bent and her ass is up in the air, pussy uncovered. "Fuck, that ass looks so good with my mark on it, but let me give it some final touches." She turns her head, watching as I beat off and nut on her ass, shooting my load onto her milky skin. With the last bit, I bend down and rub the tip on her pussy lips. She gasps and moans, jutting her little cunt out to get more.

I lean down over her, pressing my cock against her ass and my mouth near her ear. "Soon, I won't stop with my cum on the outside, Viper. It will be where it belongs. For now, you smell like me: your king, and tomorrow, your husband."

She gasps as she pushes away from me, adjusting her clothes as best as she can, being tied up. I calmly fix myself while she stares at it. I'm still semi hard and with her beautifully angry eyes on it, I'm almost hard again. She'd better be careful. I lift her panties up and put them in place.

"I'm not marrying you," she hisses, trying to bounce off the bed.

Funny, she didn't protest when I was making her come and when I sprayed my nut all over her, but marriage is a no-go.

I tap her nose. "You should have thought about that before you had me kill my capo."

"I didn't tell you to kill him."

"Wife, you were scared and in tears. Not to mention, he had his hands inside your fucking pussy."

"He didn't have his hand in there, obviously, since you couldn't even get one of your thick fingers in me."

"Good to know. So I won't have to chop off his hand and burn it before he goes to hell." I reach down and slip my finger in her hole, causing her to moan. "You sound so damn good when you're compliant."

"I'm not marrying you."

I help her to her feet. "Yes, you are. You're going to make it right because everyone will think I'll just kill for anyone." When I open the bedroom door, I find her father there. He's still one of my men. He frowns when he sees us together, but I say, "Vivian will marry me in the morning."

"The hell I am."

"Okay, you see what I can do to those who betray me, Viper. You owe me, and I won't accept anything less or I'll just have to finish off someone else." I look right at her father.

"You're a bastard."

"I'm not. I have parents. They are visiting and are downstairs."

"Yes, and they aren't pleased about Santos."

"Well, he should have kept his hands off what's mine."

He looks right at his daughter. "He put his hands on you?" her father asks, venom in his eyes. I have his daughter looking thoroughly disheveled and still tied up.

"Yes, but…I could have handled myself."

I roll my eyes. "I've already proven you can't, amore. Now go get ready for our wedding, and by the way—happy birthday." I pat her ass, knowing my seed is drying on her bottom. "Oh, I'll need this back." I untie her hands, drawing attention to my silk tie on her wrists. I don't give a fuck what I'm implying. It's all the more reason for her father to insist she marry me. For all he knows, I just bred his daughter.

"You're a bastard."

"You're asking for a repeat, amore. Go on, now. I'll see you later, Viper."

CHAPTER FOUR

VIVIAN

"What the hell happened, Vee? Are you okay?" My father looks me over, but not too closely. I'm sure he knows what happened, or at least sort of. I'm already flush from having the best orgasm in the world, but there's no doubt that my cheeks have gotten redder than my ass. Heaven help me that I can sit down properly in front of my dad.

"I'm fine, but I'm not marrying Matteo," I insist as we make our way out of the mansion and past the guards, including Matteo's parents and their anxious expressions.

His eyes slam shut, and a sigh escapes him. "I hate to ask this, but did Matteo ra...."

I cut him off before he could say something that wrong about Matteo. "No, he didn't."

"But something happened between you two?" he asks, groaning at the idea.

"Yes," I admit. Shit, something happened all right. Everything I wanted and didn't at the same time: pleasure and heartache. He's marrying me to save face with his men to avoid a freaking coup. He killed one of his men without question, and loyalties will be tested. The easiest way would be to make a statement of fact. Touching his wife was unacceptable. Something that Santos had done and paid the price for.

"Then you're marrying him," he says, walking me to the car while glaring at every guard who dares to even look at me.

"We hate each other," I insist as my father slides me into his vehicle, closing the door before without responding.

When he climbs into the driver's side, he scoffs, "Didn't look like it to me. Now, let's go home. You weren't supposed to be over here in the first place, so the fact that you were needs answering." The last they were aware I was in my bedroom doing research.

"I don't want to talk about it." It comes out in a mutter as I stare out the window, seeing nothing through my unshed tears. I wipe them away quickly so my father can't see them.

"Why the fuck was Santos on you?"

"He caught me alone and tried to hit on me." My response is flat and as a matter of fact as possible, keeping the details out of it so my father doesn't know how close it really came. If Matteo hadn't come in when he did, I don't know what would have happened. Santos had caught me so far off guard, I was trapped. Never had I been cornered like that, and he was larger than Matteo and even my father. A true goon.

"So, Matteo killed him for it?"

"Yes," I whisper.

He lets out a chuckle. "And you say he hates you." I left out the part where he heard Santos threatening to rape me with his hands on me and me pinned to Matteo's desk.

My father would have done the same as Matteo without an ounce of hesitation. Most of the guys would have pulled him off or beat the dog shit out of him because I'm my dad's daughter, but they don't have the power to do what Matteo or my dad would have done.

"It's a loyalty thing to you more than anything."

"Okay, if you say so." A text hits his phone. "So, it's on for tomorrow morning at St. Mary's."

"Are you serious?" My eyes nearly pop out of my head because that's freaking nuts. There's no way he's able to get that together so fast. Squash that, of course he's able to pull it off in a heartbeat, but it doesn't mean it's what I want. Although what I want doesn't matter right now. A part of me understands that I fucked up, but this time I hadn't walked in to cause trouble. It landed on my lap.

"Yes," my father says sternly.

"He's insane. I can't marry him." I shook my head, clamping my lips shut while crossing my arms. It may come off petulant, but this is the rest of my life and to be married to a man who only wants me as his wife because of a technicality isn't fair.

"Why not? A part of you doesn't hate him as much as you believe, and you need someone like him to keep your ass in check."

When we entered the house, we ran straight into my mother. Seeing her only reignites my emotions. She and father married out of love. They're utterly devoted to each other, and I'm supposed to marry a man who frustrates me, who thinks I'm a child, and who calls me a snake. I'm not sexy like my mother. I'm not refined, either.

"What's going on?" she questions gently, reading my frustration.

"I hate him," I hiss. "I'm going to kill him. I don't care what anyone says. Capo or not."

"Who, sweetheart?" Mom asks so sweetly, being the loving, supporting person I need. I wish I could just let my guard down and tell her the truth. Tell her that I'm tired of being me. Tell her that I'm...in love.

"Matteo," my father says, sounding annoyed.

"What happened?" Shit, my mom is worried, which is only going to irritate my father, and that means I'm in trouble and so is anyone that gets in his way.

I can't take this shit anymore because it's my birthday, and what I thought was going to be amazing has been ruined. "He's an asshole is what he is, and you're no better." I point right at my father.

"Little girl, I'd watch it or you'll be in trouble," my mom yells at me, but I don't care. Right now, I'm brokenhearted and there's nothing that will make it right.

"I'm already sentenced to a fate worse than death anyway, so whatever." I've never felt so damn on edge.

"Make sure she doesn't leave her room," I hear my father say as I storm off. "And don't stand too close. She's feeling a bit testy, and so is Matteo."

I slam my bedroom door shut, giving no fucks about the rules today. I won't be here much longer, anyway. Going through my room, I pack up my belongings because I'm supposedly getting married, but I'm not going through with it, even if it means running.

For the life of me, I can't explain how my father didn't come to my defense, but then again, I screwed up royally and created a storm in the Conti Crime Family. The death of Matteo's second will not be something people will take lightly.

How did this happen? I pull the little card out from under my pillow with tears in my eyes.

Happy birthday, my little serpent.

For years, I've longed to take you in my arms and worship you. Own that perfect figure until you're screaming for me, but the time wasn't right. Now, I can finally surrender at your feet, my little queen.

Follow these little clues and come get your special present. I know you're slippery enough to evade all the guards.

How could I have been so stupid to believe it was from Matteo? Yes, he would be the one to challenge me like this, but to confess feelings for me would be so damn foolish. He hates me almost as much as I hate him. That's what I went in there to tell him when I'd been caught off guard by that jackass.

I crept across the lawns, dodging guards, missing all the cameras, having slinked past them numerous times before. Matteo missed all the things he said before. *"You stupid bitch. He'd never want you. He might protect his favorite enforcer's little terror, but you're not the girl he'd marry. It's going to be fun to see how he failed to protect you. All that effort gone to waste."*

Matteo loved my father as his own because he was amazing at his job and I was just a pain in the ass they had to control to keep my dad happy and working for them.

I tear the stupid card in half and toss it and the rose in my trash.

With my light suitcase packed, I hear a rapid knock on my door. "Sweetheart, can I come in?" my mother asks.

"One moment." I tuck the suitcase under the bed and go to the door, opening it for her.

"Vivian, my little girl. I don't know what happened today, but I want to talk about it. Will you talk to me?"

"What is there to say? I'm marrying a man that's only doing it to save face, so he doesn't have an uprising on his hands," I say.

"It's more than that."

"Yes, he enjoys control and a challenge. I'm a challenge he wants to conquer."

She smiles, brushing her hand through my hair. "So, you know how your father and I met?"

I nod. "Dad worked for Uncle Dario, and he was in love with Aunt May."

"Yes, but that's not how we met." Now that I come to think about it, did they ever really tell us? Maybe not. Everything in this family is meant to be a secret, after all.

"How did you meet?" I huff, plopping down on my bed, waiting for her to explain.

"I kicked him in the balls when he tried to kidnap me." My eyes shoot up before she manages to finish her sentence.

"He tried to kidnap you?" Oh my goodness, I thought I got my toughness from my father, but it's not just him. Mom has a hidden side that I wasn't aware of. A real ball buster.

"Well, technically he succeeded a few minutes later, but I got in a good shot before then."

I slap my hand to my mouth, holding back a deep belly laugh. "Oh my God."

"Yes, well, I didn't even know it was him who grabbed me, so I reacted. Besides, I didn't know him anyway, and you've seen how intimidating he can appear. Imagine in the middle of the woods during a rainstorm." I just stare and shake my head. They are two crazy people who love each other unconditionally. "See? It's very complicated. When I first lived with your Aunts May and June, I worked at a news station."

"Why did you stop?"

"One, I met your father, and two...well, let's just say it wasn't the right place for me."

"So how did the whole kidnapping, ball-knocking thing happen?" I want the details. I'm old enough to know how they truly met and managed to not kill each other.

"Well, I was on assignment in Missouri with my boss, who was a total pervert, and your father stalked me all the way there."

"Stalked you?"

"Yeah, he saw a picture of me and knew I'd be his wife. He wasn't too happy that I was away with another man and lost it. In reality, he actually saved me from not only myself, but from some nasty people. I was running to some dangerous territory without proper gear and no cell phone signal in the middle of a rainy night."

"Damn."

"So we don't always see our path, but things work out. Matteo's a good man. Crazy as fuck, but in my opinion, he's perfect for you."

"Perfect for me? He doesn't have feelings for me, and what about all the whores that are after him?"

"Do you see him with any?"

"No, but that doesn't mean he isn't discreet about his private affairs."

"You don't have to worry about his fidelity to you, my sweet Vee. He respects marriage and all that it means." Maybe I won't be enough for him. Matteo is a man's man, and I'm a woman who kicks ass. Don't know how to be sexy, but my mom wouldn't understand that since she's the epitome of beauty. Even at her age, she outshines me by miles. My dad worships the ground she walks on. That's a love I want, an obsession I crave, and there's only one man I want it all from. He's just not up for the task.

"I just can't. Mom, I need to be left alone."

"Okay. Just think about what I said. You do find him handsome, don't you?"

"Of course—everyone does."

"That's the problem, isn't it?"

"What, Mom?"

"You don't feel like you can compete with other women?"

"No. I'm not sexy. I've been the tough one."

"Sweetheart, you wear tight clothes to exact your strikes, and you have a killer body. You are more than sexy, and I have no doubt that Matteo not only notices, but he also appreciates it very much. Now, if you'd like, we can pick a perfect dress for tonight's party and prove it."

"I don't have a great dress for tonight." I had planned on wearing a sexy pantsuit, but I want to look drop-dead gorgeous, and suddenly the thought of Matteo sliding his hands under my dress has merit. It's silly, considering he's only marrying me to save face, but in that brief moment, I felt the chemistry. The deep, animalistic kiss, the way he sucked off his fingers and threatened to mark me as his.

"Well, then, we'll go shopping."

"Okay. Give me twenty minutes to shower and change."

"I'll be waiting downstairs." My mother pats my thigh and leaves my room.

It gives me a moment to compose myself and consider her words. Still, it's not enough to make me change my plans. Tonight, there will be at least five other men here, looking to gain me as an asset to their families. Unlike Matteo, I don't have feelings for them, so their bargaining chips will be easier to deal with. They want a wife, but they know who I am and what I bring to the table.

Frankly, until my change of heart, I never considered marrying for anything other than power. If Matteo has claimed me as his, how will tonight go?

I keep my suitcase from being seen and then I head into the bathroom for a quick shower. Once I wash Matteo's scent off my body, I dress in a pair of tight shorts and a tank top with a light sweater. The weather is a strange mix, hot yet breezy. Once I put on my sneakers and tie my dark curls up in a ponytail, I meet my mother in the foyer.

"Mrs. Conti," I gasp, seeing her standing at the door with my mother.

"I thought it was best that May goes with us." What are they cooking up between them? Sometimes I wonder if I get some of my antics from my mother.

"And since when has it been Mrs. Conti?" she says, frowning at me.

"Since your son just changed the rules of engagement," I bite off. My eyes shoot to the side, glaring at my future husband who has decided to pop up beside his mother, looking innocent when we all know that he's the devil reincarnate.

"Interesting choice of words, my little Viper." My heart doubles its pace when he calls me that with such a growly tone. Giving me a once-over, Matteo's voice deepens. "You changed." His eyes narrow, and he approaches me too damn boldly for his own good. He knows I'm always armed. If our mothers weren't here, I'd show him his viper.

Matteo lowers his head, his scent filling my nostrils, and I don't miss my scent all over him still. There's something dirty and needy running through me, knowing he didn't bother to clean up afterward. "I might have to spank you again for washing me off."

"Matteo," I hiss, looking past him toward our mothers wondering if they heard him, but they seemed to have left the room. In fact, it looks like they left the house.

"Eyes over here, Viper," he commands, gripping my chin and turning my head to face him. "They gave us a moment."

"We don't need a moment," I tell him. Everything we have to say can be said in front of others, where I feel a lot less vulnerable, less horny. No, that's a lie. We could be in a crowd of a thousand people and if he's near me, I'm a messy puddle.

He straightens his spine and glares at me. "Must you be a pain in the ass?" I'm getting on his nerves and I'm enjoying it a little too much.

"Says the man who enjoyed spanking mine." His lips twist into an upward smirk, making him even more devilishly handsome.

"Yes, and so did you. It must be why you decided it was smart to wash off my scent and then plan to head outside where there are other men aching to touch you." There's something in his tone that tells me he's seriously angry. Even with the hint of a smile, the tension is evident in his body. "Do you want men eye fucking what's mine, knowing that I'm capable of putting a bullet in them if they lay a hand on you?"

I'm reminded of this morning and the damage done by sneaking over to the property. "No, I get it. You're the head of the mafia and you have a point to prove, but so do I. I can't try on dresses all dirty. They will go back on the rack to someone else." It's something that popped in my head, but now that it's there the thought of his seed on another woman doesn't sit well with me at all, and I'm more agitated than before.

"Fine, amore." Did he just call me that? I ignore it. I heard it earlier, but we were in the throes of passion. "Then you will wear this." He slides a heavy yellow diamond ring on my finger. "This is for my wife." It's a beautiful ring, opulent and stunning.

"It's beautiful, but it's not for me." I grasp it with my other hand, but he quickly places his hands over mine, stopping me immediately.

"Don't fucking dare take this off."

I glare at him suspiciously. "It has a tracker in it, doesn't it?" The bastard. I wonder how he got it so fast. Who was this ring for? Well, I have average-size fingers.

"I don't need one when it comes to you." Oh, I forgot. I'm not that important. A means to an end. He protected me on principle, not because I meant anything to him.

"Of course, so if you'll excuse me, I have to get a dress for tonight."

"Don't you have one for this evening?"

"It's called retail therapy. I know it's hard to fathom, but marrying you isn't something I'm looking forward to doing, so I need to enjoy some time away." A slow smile spreads over his face, but then I sense something else I can't read.

"Go on, amore. I'll enjoy seeing what you've selected. Don't forget to buy something sexy for our wedding night. I want to see you in clothes I plan to tear off with my teeth." He pops me on my ass with his palm, catching me off guard. "Get going before I forget all my plans and take you to your room, putting my scent all over you. Everyone will know you belong to me, Vivian."

His phone rings in his pocket. "Excuse me. Have fun." He walks away without another word, stepping back outside and to his waiting car.

I walk out of the house with my emotions a complete wreck. "Oh, my goodness, Vee. That ring is beautiful," my mother says, spotting the ring as soon as I climb into the back of the waiting limo.

"Thanks. Mom," I say, feeling the weight of the ring and Matteo's reminder not to take it off.

Matteo's mother hasn't said a word about the ring, but that is because she's on the phone with her husband, who I'm sure is giving his warning about her safety for the hundredth time even though there is plenty of security going with us. We never leave without a handful of guards. Well, I escape sometimes on my own, but no one knows about that.

CHAPTER FIVE

MATTEO

I STORM BACK INTO MY HOUSE AND INTO MY office where the mess of earlier has been cleaned up. No one would know that my second-in-command once lay on the floor in a pool of blood.

"A word, Matteo," my father says behind me.

"Yes, Father. Please close the door." He shuts it as I stare at the desk, violently shoving it out of the way. "I want this fucking thing out of here before Vivian comes back here." It makes me sick to even see it there. A reminder of what transpired earlier.

He walks over to the sideboard and fills up two glasses of whiskey before handing me one. "What happened?" he questioned, not as the mob boss he was, but as my father.

"I'm not sure why she was here, but he had her pinned to my desk, attempting to rape her. She was in tears trying to fight him off."

The sound of his glass cracking doesn't miss my ears as he barks out, "What?"

"Yes. And when I asked him about it, he dared to tell me they were having a discussion. So you see why I fucking put a hole in his head." I could barely contain the anger in my voice as I let the words out. The memory so new and fresh replayed and I wanted to kill him all over again.

"Are you sure that's not what you wanted to see?" Seriously, did he just say that?

I lowered the glass I had finished from my lips and twisted my head. For the first time in forever, lose my temper with the man I respect most in this world. "Father, you're so fucking lucky that nothing happened to her because I'm on the verge of snapping. I heard what he told her as he threatened to take her."

"I'm just making sure."

"That my men don't want to jump ship because I killed my second? Hell, they know they don't cross me. He crossed me, and if anyone else does, they'll meet the same consequences. It isn't that fucking hard."

"That's understandable. I just wanted to make sure you weren't just being jealous because it could cost us a lot in the long run." Jealousy had nothing to do with what happened. All I saw was my future wife being assaulted and that wasn't going to go down.

"Of course not. At least not in that fucking moment," I shake my head back and forth. Pouring myself another shot of whiskey, I drink it down quickly, slamming the glass on the desk.

"Then we'll burn this desk. Do you know why she was in here?" he asked. It's the same question I had, but getting answers out of Vivian could lead to tying her ass down for them. As much as I'd like to see her compliant, I'm not picking a fight with her stubborn ass.

"No. She refused to tell me."

He chuckled and finished his drink, setting it on the desk. "Damn, you have your hands full with her."

"Tell me about it." I smile because I'm anticipating the challenge. "Now let me call my men in for a brief meeting. I want to address the situation correctly before anyone gets out of hand and rumors fly."

"Good. I have your back, as always. So do your brothers."

I truly appreciate his support because at this transition phase everyone is going to be watching my actions and my father's reactions to them. "Thank you."

"It's not what I wanted to happen today, but this will be your first test as the head of the family. I'm proud of you either way, son." He pulls me in for a hug. "Now let's conquer this problem head on."

We step outside of my office, and he says, "Mando, go in and clear out the desk. We want it burned. Completely destroyed."

"Yes, Don Dario." They still treat my father with the respect that he deserves even though I'm the new head of the family.

"Summon all the men into the meeting area in the next five minutes as well," I say. Mando nods and gets to work on my situation.

Less than five minutes later, we lock down the mansion and all of my men, including Enrico, are gathered in the meeting area. As much as I wanted him to be here, I don't as well. His presence makes part of this conversation sketchy. "Men, I've summoned you here today because tomorrow, I'll be marrying Vivian Barone." They all begin clapping and cheering. I raise my hand. "Calm down. There's more."

I take a deep, calming breath. "As you know, I take the safety and well-being of our family very seriously, so it must have come as a surprise that I took out a man I trusted and considered a friend, my best friend for many years. However, it was not without merit. Santos decided to touch what wasn't his. He threatened to harm my future wife. I walked in on him with his hands on her throat, choking her as he promised to violate her."

Every single man in the room became visibly angry, including her father. All eyes moved to him of course as they should. His rage was as justifiable as mine.

"Men, as you can see, that's not something that would ever be tolerated. I won't allow disrespect to my wife, let alone someone putting their hands on her. Even before I made it clear that Vivian is mine, she's Enrico's daughter and deserves respect, like everyone's daughter does. He crossed a line that was unacceptable."

"I should have pissed on his body," a voice came from the crowd.

"He deserves to rot," comes another.

Enrico comes forward and says, "We need to have a word." I nodded. The tone in his voice meant that this wasn't up for debate.

"Thank you, men. Also, that means no one touches my wife in any manner," I say, giving them a final warning.

They all respond with a cacophony of "yes" and "we understand."

My father, Enrico and I head back to my office, and we sit down. "So, she didn't tell me what the fuck happened when I asked. He didn't just flirt with her."

"No. He had his hands on her. Do you know what she was doing in my office? She's never been in here unless you were here."

"No, she was in her bedroom researching her potential suitors for the night."

"What the fuck do you mean, 'suitors'?" I'm ready to crush skulls as it is, so this only makes the day twice as fucked. The idea that she wants to be with any of these men pisses me off to a new level. I get that she believes an alliance is a good thing, but if she wanted anyone else but me, there would be a war, and I'd still claim her ass.

"All the guys coming to the party," Enrico added.

I scoffed at that problem, considering I'd already taken control of the situation. "That was a pointless endeavor because I sent them a message that she's mine before I found her in my office."

"Couldn't wait?" My future father-law crosses his arms and stares at me with suspicion.

"No, just trying to stop a war before it started, but I had no idea that she'd come here. What was she looking for? She doesn't need to research me."

"No. In fact, she said the Conti Family men were off the table, so I'm not sure why she was here. Something changed in the short time she was in her room."

"I think that bastard tricked her into coming here," my father says. I hadn't considered the idea. So much has taken place today that I haven't thought straight for more than five fucking minutes.

"Do you think so?" Enrico asked.

I consider his guess, and it makes sense. "Well, it's possible. Vivian had no reason to come over here on her birthday, into my office unless she was planning on seducing me, which you know damn well she wasn't," I muttered.

"Does it really matter?" My father asks, wondering if it changes how I feel about her.

"No, but it's on my mind." Vivian's always on my mind and this wasn't something small. I roll my shoulders back, trying to loosen up the tension flowing through me.

"Do you really think she wanted to meet up with him?" Enrico questions, staring at me like I'm delusional.

I tilt my head and crack my neck. That thought would never ever be acceptable to me. The image of his hands on her soft, slender body, caressing her, loving on her while Vivian enjoyed it would kill me.

"Not for a tryst, but maybe for a job. She's always trying to prove herself," I answer. The violence I witnessed earlier with Santos, and the way she creamed in my arms proved just that. She didn't want him sexually, so their meeting was something else.

My father rubs his chin and asks, "Yes, son, but why your office, of all places? You know damn well that she wouldn't have come here if she was trying to go on assignment."

It takes me a moment to think about it and then a thought hits me. "Not unless she thought I was the one summoning her here."

"It's possible."

"I need to get back before the women do. I have party stuff I'm assigned to handle while she deals with Vivian. Are you sure my little girl is okay?" Enrico questioned, being the doting father he has always been.

"As far as the incident, I think so. When it comes to marrying me, she has her reservations, but I'll work on her. She's not as completely indifferent to me as I thought." Something about us is bothering her, but I won't let it get in the way.

"No, just maybe you two should talk a bit more." I get his meaning completely. So I should keep my dick out of her when I'm talking to her, but he doesn't know I understand my woman, love her with everything I am. It drives me nuts how intense my love is for her. No one could even fathom the depth.

"After the wedding. I want her as mine. It's not just my men that I want to make understand she's under my protection. We have enemies, and she's safer as my wife than my fiancée."

"You're right about that." Things have been quiet for far too long, and today's incident just brings me to the realization that she's not as safe as I'd like. I'd wrap her up in bubble wrap or tie her to my bed to keep her secure, but that would never make me happy. Her crazy is part of the reason I fell madly in love with her.

"We'll double the security around the houses," I say.

Enrico's phone goes off. "Son of a bitch. January's mad." He stares at me with a slow sneer spreading over his face. "Strangely, I've had two cancelations for tonight."

"Really?" I say, smirking over my own success.

"Yes, two of the single Bianchi boys who were planning on coming together, and Landon Black's sons."

"Damn, can't imagine why," I say, my grin growing. The hell if I want to have other men ogling my woman even if things are set in stone as far as I'm concerned. They're great allies and I'd hate to mop the floor with their faces.

"What exactly did you tell them?" my father asked, trying to stave off a laugh.

"I'm marrying Vivian so they can go find a wife elsewhere, but they are welcome to some food and drink. Maybe a congratulations."

"I think you're going to need to bring your future mother-in-law a wedding present instead of the other way around," my father teases.

"I'll think of something she'd like and let you know," Enrico mutters before leaving my office.

My father and I stare at each other, knowing damn well this could go sideways if I piss off Mrs. Barone because all our moms are tight and as thick as thieves.

"I wish you all the best, my boy. You make me proud because I thought your mother was a handful," he says, clapping my shoulder before walking out of my office. Now to prepare for the woman I'm obsessed with. My viper isn't going to know what hit her.

CHAPTER SIX

MATTEO

I ARRIVE IN TIME TO GREET MY BRIDE-TO-BE, only to find she's not downstairs yet. "Well, if it's not the man who's marrying my sister," her older brother says, coming up to me with a firm handshake.

"Hello, Giovanni. How are you? Where's Marco?" I haven't seen her other older brother Marco yet. It's been a week or so. He's like his father for sure, sneaky and dangerous, but no one is as bad as my Vivian.

"Good. He's around here somewhere. Are you sure you want to marry Vee?" he says with a wink. He's probably worried about my sanity or hers. We could be on an episode of Wives with Knives if I'm not careful, but I'm looking forward to the pleasure of having Vivian at my side. Even if she's holding a blade to it.

"Without a doubt," I answered with no hesitation in my voice.

"Awesome. She's my sister and if anyone can handle her, it's you." I nod and walk away, looking around to find my woman. She's not down after a bit, but I wait a little longer, meeting with others, including her parents who give me a warm reception.

"Matteo, it's so good to see you," Mrs. Barone, my Aunt January, like I would normally call her, but soon she'll be my mother-in-law. Of course, as the head of the family, I don't catch flak from them even though I'm planning to take away their daughter.

"It's wonderful to see you. Did you get the flowers I sent?" I had them rushed over after my talk with Enrico.

"Yes, they are lovely, but you didn't need to make up for tonight."

"Wife, don't lie. You had everything planned down to the number of glasses wine we planned to serve."

"As bad as I should feel, I don't have any reservations about warning away any men. Speaking of reservations, our guest of honor hasn't arrived."

"Give her time. She's had a rough day."

I nodded and excused myself. Still, as the minutes tick by, my temper grows short. It takes all the strength I have to stand back and let her play this game with me. She's late to come down to the party. We all know damn well it started twenty minutes ago, and the guests have begun to arrive.

Since there's no need for delay, I make a point to tell every man here that she's mine long before the event. However, the birthday party has now turned into an engagement party, and without the guest of honor, it's pointless.

"Congratulations, and may I say—good luck," Luca Bianchi says, smirking with his hand on his wife's waist. He's two years older than me and recently married. The love between them is clear and so is his possessiveness.

"I'll need it," I grumbled, looking up toward the stairs.

"Boys, I'll help her if you keep this up," his wife says.

"Oh, no. I better hold my tongue. The two of them together could be dangerous." I smile, knowing he's not wrong, but at least there is someone out there who my wife could be allies with.

"If you'll excuse me, I need to retrieve my bride before she changes her mind." I wink and then exit the room.

Most believe that I took my family protection to the next level, but they have no idea that I'd staked my claim on her before they had a chance. After this afternoon, she is completely mine and no one else will have a chance to come after my woman, and everyone tonight knows it.

Although there are guards nearby, I didn't want them right outside her door after what happened today. Approaching, I ask, "Has Vivian exited?"

"No, Ms. Barone hasn't left her room." I knock, because even though she'll be my wife soon, it would be too much to just storm in there.

She doesn't answer, so I knock again. "Vivian, open the door." Pissed, I grab the handle, and it's locked. My phone is already out of my suit jacket, so I pulled up the surveillance app, and I spot her still in her room. She wants to play this game with me.

"I'll fix that," I mutter to myself.

"Sorry, boss. Did you say something?"

"No. Excuse me." I pulled out a special kit that I had a feeling I'd need. I pop the lock on her door and go inside, propping a chair under the handle to stop anyone from trying to come in. She's not in the room which makes me fucking nervous. If she got rid of the damn bracelet on her hand and the one on her necklace, I'm going to spank her ass. As I peer around the room, I hear some fiddling in her closet. I whip it open, and I spot her trying to sneak through a tiny crawl space. She's too slow for me, though.

With quick hands, I snatch her little ass up and drag her out. "Going somewhere, my viper?" I state, pulling her firmly to her waist.

"Let me go, asshole," she hisses through clenched teeth.

"Never." She's kicking her legs at me, but I hold them tightly before tossing her on the bed and then pinning her down with my entire weight. She tries to fight me, but I grab her wrists in one hand and hold them above her head. "I feel like we've been here before," I say, breathing heavy, dick jerking against her thigh.

"Yes, but this time we have guests waiting for us," she says as if she gave a fuck about them a minute ago.

"Exactly—that makes it even better. The idea of every man down there knowing you're covered in my scent only gets me harder." I grind my hips on her, wanting her to understand how serious I am.

"Are you an animal?" She attempts to sound offended, but her voice comes out half aroused with very little bite.

"I thought you knew that already, baby." I crushed my mouth to hers, kissing her violently. She pretends to protest, but it only lasts a moment before she's moaning and parting her lips, allowing me entrance, which I gladly take, delving my tongue inside. Our kiss isn't brief and it's filled with pure hunger.

My mouth moves along her jaw, nipping on her chin and down to her throat. "Amore, mine." Our hips naturally grind, and I want to fucking tear off her clothes and fill her this second, but she's right. There are guests downstairs. If we fuck now, I'll never let her get away to celebrate her birthday and I'm already on Aunt January's bad side. When I let her get away earlier, it had been hard as hell. I wanted to pull her in and make love to her until neither of us saw straight.

"Vivian, we need to head downstairs," I say, breathing some rational thought between us.

"Of course. It would help if you got your big old body off me," she says, pushing me off her. It's cute that she's bothered, but I don't want her really upset.

"Don't get mad at me because you're still horny, Viper. Look what you did to me." I press my hand to the painful erection in my pants.

Her pretty eyes widen, and her filthy mouth falls open. "Shit. You can't go downstairs like that." Damn she's flush and her hair is messy after our little encounter. That smart mouth of hers is all puffy from the abuse it just received, stiffening my erection.

"Of course, I can't because walking has just gotten painful. Besides, your father wouldn't be too pleased," I grumbled, trying to think of anything else. My mind goes to what happened this morning with Santos and it's like a bucket of ice down my pants.

"All the whores would be," she huffs out under her breath, revealing that my little viper is jealous.

"Luckily, I don't give a fuck about anyone else. You made it this way, and you're the only one who will fix it. Whether it's with that bad-girl mouth of yours or that tight little pussy, soon you'll take care of my needs."

"What if I don't want to?" Damn she always wants to fight.

"I'll persuade you," I say, cupping her chin roughly.

"How?" Quickly, I drop my head and brush my face against her hot pussy and bite down on her cunt, causing her to moan. When I pull away, she presses her thighs together, biting down on her bottom lip and glaring at me with a flushed face. "Fucking bastard."

"See, bad girl? You want what I want. Now, be a good fiancée and get dressed."

"I can't get dressed with you in here," she complains as if that's going to change anything. I'll strip her out of her clothes and slide new ones on if I have to. There's no way in hell, I'm giving her an inch of space.

"I sure as fuck am not letting you play that game with me. Besides, if you're a good girl, I'll give you a birthday present." Her eyes open up wide, and she pops off the bed.

She winks. "I don't want to disappoint my parents, anyway."

"That's what I thought." I see the dress on the back of the closet door and groan. It's a one-shoulder, skin-tight black number that's probably only going to hit the bottom of her ass. This is going to be a long—or a very short—night. "Undress."

"Bossy." I close the distance between us again, leaving just breathing room, and fist her long hair, tipping her head upward.

"That's what I am, baby. I'm the boss. Don't forget that shit. Now undress, so I can give you a present before we greet your guests." I kiss her lips softly and pull back, watching her eyes get fuzzy with desire. My thumb runs over her bottom lip. "I can't wait for you to receive your present."

She takes off her top, and her tits bounce in a tight, lacy black bra. I lick my lips and lean against the door to watch the show.

Fuck me. Cum leaks from the tip, coating my silk boxers. They are trash for sure. Why I bothered to wear them was stupid. Then again, I wasn't thinking straight at all.

"Like what you see?" That's my woman, bringing the sexy sass.

"You know I do." I grip my cock through my pants, letting her see the full length that's going to be buried inside her later. She blushes and kicks off her shoes and then pulls down her leggings, taking her socks with them. She's only wearing a pair of black panties and bra, leaving me salivating, but as promised, I want to give her a present: that orgasm she needs.

I took her hand and led her over to the bed. I lay down and say, "Come here, Viper. Come ride my face." I want her to fuck my beard.

"What?" She's immediately shy again, but I'm not having it.

"You heard me. Bring me that pussy over here. I want you to come and get what you need."

"Is that my present?" she asks.

"Yes, baby. I can't have you going down there with that pussy all needy." She climbs up on the bed, straddling my face with her panties on. Fuck, I'm so aroused, I'm going to nut in my pants like a pubescent. I breathe in her heat, getting my fill. She slides the lace out of the way to give me those plump, slick, juicy lips.

"Fuck, show me whose pussy this is. Feed me." She puts her hot cunt on my mouth, and then I press my tongue into her wetness, and she cries out, slapping her hand over her mouth while I hold her up by her round ass. Unintelligible words escape both of us as I devour her slit.

She grinds her snatch all over my mouth and I can't get enough.

"Matteo," she cries out. Her ass flexes as she creams all over my face, riding her orgasm out like a rodeo. I slap that ass several times, loving the feel of it as it jiggles in my hands. I can't wait until I fill her up. Gripping her waist, I flip her off me and onto the mattress.

"You're so sexy, Vivian." I reach down and adjust her panties, putting them back in place before spanking her mound.

"You enjoy spanking me." I shrug because it's true.

"You need it. It's been a long time coming." I held out my hand for her to take, helping her stand up.

"I could spend a long time coming," she adds.

I pull her in for a kiss, but I quickly break it before I flip her onto the bed and stuff my dick so deep inside of her. She's too damn responsive for me and I'm hooked. "We will soon, but get dressed so we can meet everyone."

"We know everyone." She rolls her eyes, and I feel her pain. I want to stay up here between her legs, losing ourselves with orgasm after orgasm while I fill her with little ones.

"Yes, but not as my fiancée," I insist. Everyone needs to understand that she belongs to me.

"What's going on?" She points to my hard-on, which disappeared.

"Baby, let's just say we finished together. Put your dress on, and I'll clean up." She smiles, and it's a genuine one. She picked up the dress off the closet door, and then I head into the bathroom. Luckily, you can't see my nut through my suit. That would be a little embarrassing. I toss the towel on the counter, and it falls on the floor. When I pick it up, I spot a card and a rose in the garbage.

When I bring the ripped card up, I push the two pieces together and read.

*My little serpent...*those damn words send me into a rage. Everything clicks in my brain, and this morning makes a lot more damn sense. Taking a calming breath before I tear apart this place and dig up his body to kill him all over again, I remember that there are about a hundred people waiting for us to reappear.

Tucking the card into my suit jacket, I step outside the bathroom and find her slipping on her shoes. She lifts her gaze, and her beautiful eyes are a mix of nervousness and something I can't read. Vivian has a toughness that makes her scared to be vulnerable, and today she was out of her element. Still, she gave herself to me, orgasming so effortlessly.

Now, she's going to face another round of surprises.

She stands, and I'm floored. The dress was made for her, and I swear my mother did this to torture me. "This dress is going to have me killing someone tonight."

"Why?"

"Because you're mine, and men are going to be staring."

"I doubt it." There's that undercurrent of sadness that tears at my chest.

"Come here." I snatch her by the wrist and pull her to me, letting her feel my length. "You see what you're already doing to me? I'm stiff again."

"What are we going to do? You can't go down there like that," she gasps, shaking her head.

"It will calm down in a minute."

"I don't want anyone seeing you like that."

"Says the woman who looks so fucking delectable with her tits and ass almost popping out of her dress."

"Matteo, do you like my dress?" she questions, running her hand up my dress shirt.

"I prefer you out of it." I wag my brows. "Tomorrow I'll show you just how much when I stuff my fat cock deep inside of you. Now enough of this, my viper. Let us go and greet our guests."

"Fine, but later we'll continue this." I swear, I sense that she thinks this is a game and that I'm not serious about it. Like I would go around messing with her and then leave her for someone else. She acts like she's unworthy, but it couldn't be further from the truth. Soon, she'll grasp what she means to me.

"With pleasure," I say, bringing her hand up to my lips and kissing the back of it.

Just as we open the bedroom door there's a loud boom rocking somewhere outside.

"Sir, go back in," my guard says, taking off to run toward the noise.

Slamming the door shut, I grab my woman and drag her back to her crawl space. "Fuck, let's go."

"My parents," she cries out, she heads toward the bedroom door, but I drag her back.

"We'll get to them. I promise. My family is downstairs too." I don't think it's for them, anyway. This was meant for us. Fuck me. I should have known better and listened to them when they wanted to cancel the party.

We reach the hidden tunnel and burrow out of the house to a side entrance where we find a bunch of our guards having a shootout with Moreno's men. Of course, they decided to strike now on my girl's eighteenth birthday as payback.

"Don't go out there, Matteo," Vivian pleads, gripping my bicep. The fear in her voice almost makes me stay back, but I'd never let these bastards get to my family.

Turning around, I cup her face and stare into those eyes that live in my dreams. "Baby, I have to. You have to stay here until I know it's safe. Please, do this for me. For once in your life, listen to me." I kiss her hard as fuck and take off.

She's protected by her secret spot and I fucking regret not letting her run, but then again, they might have nabbed her ass trying to leave the gates. Whoever did this had to have help from inside. There's no way this party wasn't secure. Every guest was checked before allowed entry. Given that there were only a handful of guests that weren't already family, we were supposed to be secure. *Fuck.*

Always strapped, I run around the corner of the house and see our men shooting at two vehicles that barged through the front of Enrico's driveway, trapping all the guest vehicles.

Everything is a mess. The Morenos came to fight, but they fucked up because we have the Bianchis on our side, and they mean business. No one got near their women. Whoever betrayed us did a damn good job, but it has to be someone at the front gates because that's the only way to let the guests in.

"Matteo," my father calls out. "Thank God." He's panting, covered in blood spatter.

"Where's everyone?" I asked, looking around for my family and Vivian's, but only seeing some of our men.

"All the women and children are in the safety bunker. We've eliminated the threat. Where's Vivian?" he asked, peeking around me.

"I have to get her. She's hiding in her secret spot."

Not waiting for my father to keep up, I rush back to where my woman is supposed to be hiding. Just as I pull up to her, she shouts, "No."

I freeze, only to find one of the front gate guards with a gun pointed dead center of chest. I'm too fucking late;

he's mere feet away, and I'm going to die. I take a fleeting glance at the woman I love to say goodbye, but my little viper isn't one to give up. She pulls out a blade and shanks him in the neck just as he fires. The bullet grazes me, and I go down. *God, I'm in love.*

CHAPTER SEVEN

VIVIAN

THE SOUNDS AROUND THE HOUSE SET MY TEETH on edge. I slip inside the passageway and scoop out the blade I have stashed there for safety purposes and hide it in my dress. Fuck, what a terrible time to be wearing a dress and heels. If I had time, I would have tossed on sneakers and camo pants. As soon as my feet hit the grass, I hear footsteps behind me.

Spinning around, I see Philo. His appearance isn't the kind and polite man I would see often. Instead, he has a menacing sneer on his face as he approaches me. "Well, well, well. You stupid bitch. Did you think your little getaway would work? You're the one we're after. The boss's bitch."

Did he just call me a bitch twice? "You're a fool. Matteo's going to kill you."

"I'm not worried about him. He's a pussy. What kind of mafia boss turns down premium pussy to chase after a tomboy?" That shit hits me in the chest almost as much as if he shot me.

"What are you talking about?" I asked, wanting to find out who he was supposed to marry.

"It doesn't matter. You're a dead bitch, but not until we get what we want from him, and I get a safe distance away."

"Why are you doing this? Didn't we take care of you and your family?" I questioned.

"I don't have a family anymore. My wife left me when I couldn't get her sister a date with Matteo's weak ass. I hate him, and you. Fuck, I should just put a bullet in his head, and then my wife will see that I'm more of a man since I took out the head of the Conti Family." God, what a pussy. She doesn't respect him because he's a chump.

"You're fucking delusional," I exclaimed.

"Am I?" I watch his head turn, and I see the love of my life heading this way fast as hell.

Screaming, I ran at the bastard, pulling out my hidden blade. We both fall, but he gets his shot off. As he gurgles in his own blood, I dash off to Matteo and the people running to him, including our dads.

"Viper, come here," he growls out through the pain. With his left arm, he pulls me on top of him and kisses me hard.

I break off our kiss to yell at him. "You better not die on me." Tears fall from my eyes as I look over my man, who is bleeding a lot.

He chuckles. "I'm not, baby. We have a wedding tomorrow. I need my deadly queen by my side." He cups my ass and pulls me tighter so I land on him.

"Son, we're going to have to hold off on that. You're not going anywhere for a bit."

"The hell we aren't. I want Viper as mine. Now." He tenses up, glaring at his father.

"We can get married without a big wedding." I press my hand to his chest, wanting my man to relax.

"Let's get him inside," his father says. Matteo attempts to stand on his own, but his father and mine help him to his feet.

"Don't get too far from me," he says, staring at me over his father's shoulder.

"Always so bossy." I wink at him.

"I have her," my dad says, hugging me. "Come on, my little killer." He kisses the top of my head.

"How is everyone else?" I ask my father. I'd been momentarily distracted by Matteo's injury, but that doesn't mean I forgot about my family and friends.

"Everyone is safe for now. The threat isn't over, and not by far. We stopped the main threat of a bomb just outside the house. They planned to get into the secured area with the women, and that's what you heard go off."

"Oh God." My hand goes to my mouth.

"Yes, but we're glad you two got out." My father eyes me suspiciously. He knows about my secret spot.

"I'm not running anymore," I reassure him.

"Good, because you'd be making a silly mistake. Matteo would chase you down and bring you right back," he says with disgruntled chuckle.

"Sounds like fun," I say, rubbing my hands together.

"Don't start, Viper," Matteo growls from in front of us. We make it inside our house and to the living room where the doctor, who is one of our guests, prepares his medical supplies.

"Everyone can wait outside," he tells us.

"I'm going to check on your mother and the rest of the women," my father says.

"Please tell my wife that Matteo is doing well. I'll be there soon, but I'm not leaving him."

"Father, you can go with Mother if you want," Matteo grunts through the pain, presenting a strong front.

"No, I'm here by your side until I'm sure you're good." No one could deny that Dario Conti wasn't a great father who loved his kids.

"Do you want me to leave?" I ask. I don't really want to leave, but I ask just in case he's in too much pain and doesn't want me to see him weakened.

A snarling growl comes from him. "You aren't going anywhere, woman. I'm not letting you out of my sight for a very long time. You better get used to it." He kisses my lips and then looks at the doctor. "Are you ready?"

"Let's get this off you." They remove Matteo's suit jacket, tie, and shirt that are now covered in blood. I let out a gasp. I haven't seen him without a shirt since the one shootout and this time, his chest, right by his heart, is covered in the most beautiful tattoo I've ever seen: a green and black snake with honey eyes wrapped around a heart.

I pounced on my fiancé and kissed him, jolting the doctor with the surgical needle in his hand. A round of coughing floats through the room, and Matteo smiles against my lips. "Amore, he needs to finish." All this time I'd been worried about the reason he wanted to marry me, and I was way off. I had his heart. There was no mistaking that.

I sit back on my haunches beside the sofa as they get to work. "Whatever. Stop being a baby." He growls and stares at me like he's going to punish me, and I might just be getting excited for it. My world just got a lot brighter. This was real.

When they finally finish with his wound, he says, "Everyone, please leave us alone for a moment. I will meet with you all soon to handle this situation."

"You need your rest. We will gather the dead and assess the damage, son." Dario takes the lead as if he never gave up his role as the Don.

"I will be there soon, Father. I will not allow this to go unanswered." Goodness, why am I so freaking turned on by the sound of fire in Matteo's voice?

"Understood." He nods and everyone leaves the room, giving us a bit of privacy.

"So, what the fuck was that shit, baby girl? Did you call me a baby?" he asks, tilting his head, glaring at me before his sinister expression twists into a smirk.

I turn pink as my body heats up. "What are you going to do about it?"

"Teach you a fucking lesson for talking shit in front of my men." He flips me onto my belly, pulling my dress up and swatting my ass.

"Be careful with your arm," I hiss, turning my head to bitch at him like the wife he's about to get.

"It's fine." He lifts me up and sits me on his lap, holding me close. "It's my heart that's fucking aching right now, Vivian. I could have lost you today." He presses my face to his chest and I breathe him in, listening to the rapid pace of his heartbeats.

Has this man lost more than some blood? I stare at him and press my hand to his forehead to check his temperature. It seems normal. "What? I'm the one who could have lost you."

He lightly chuckles, kissing my hand. "No, I'm talking from the start of the day." He scoops up his jacket off the chair and digs into the inside pocket, pulling out the card I disposed of in my trash. "Before you get pissed, I wasn't snooping. I found this in the trash when I dropped my towel earlier."

Dropping my head, face flush with embarrassment, I confess my shame. "I thought it was from you."

He tips my chin up so my eyes meet his. "I wish it was. Santos knew about my tattoo, what I called you, and what you meant to me." Slowly he takes my mouth in a soft kiss that's healing. I adjust my body so I'm straddling his thick, muscular thighs.

"They all do. The Morenos—that's why they were here tonight. They wanted to use me to get to you." I explained what Philo had said to me before Matteo appeared.

"Fuck, I'm so sorry." He slams his eyes shut in shame, but this isn't his fault.

I cup his cheeks and make him look at me. His beautiful eyes are full of love. Something I hadn't recognized before. "Don't be sorry. We got this. I'm not some weak woman who is afraid to face them. I'm only afraid of losing you."

"Not going to happen. I'll always come back. If not in this lifetime, then in the next because you're mine, Viper. You've been mine." His mouth crushes mine as he fists my hair.

I pull my mouth back long enough to express my needs. "Show me. I need you, Matteo."

"There's no going back from this," he tells me.

"Was there really ever?" I questioned.

"No, you were always meant to be mine, even before I knew it myself." His mouth brushes down my jaw and to my throat, sucking and licking until I'm bending and arching to give him more access to me. The hem of my dress rides up, and he lets out a grunt. "Fuck, I'm not going to last."

"Please," With a twirl of his tongue, he laves it over my chest, lowering the strapless side down and freeing my breast.

"So perfect." My breath catches as he snatches my nipple into his hot mouth.

"Yes, Matteo." I bite down on my bottom lip, rolling my hips forward.

He suddenly lifts me off the chair, covering me up. "It's time to go to bed."

"No, but…"

"Viper, calm down. I'm not taking you in the living room where anyone can walk in, including your dad. We're going upstairs where I can breed your virgin womb with our next generation." He carries me up to my bedroom, avoiding most of the guards.

"No one disturbs us. Go find something to do down the hall." I blush because they know he's going to fuck me.

I pop out of his hold and stand in the middle of my room. "You want to put a baby in me?"

"Of course. I've been thinking about it for way longer than I should have. If I could have, I would have punished you two years ago and bent you over those pallets that day and stuffed my dick deep inside you so you'd keep that pussy where it belongs, in the house warm and ready for me when I'm done with business."

"And after you're done with your whores?" I dared to ask. None of the other men in our family were like that, but I wanted confirmation.

"No need for jealousy, baby girl. When I bust that little barrier with my big cock, you'll be the only woman to know what my dick feels like."

"What?"

"I hadn't planned on waiting, but bloodlust was all I was after until my need to protect you shifted. Now, enough talking." He takes off the rest of his clothes while I stand and watch. "Get naked, or I'll tear that dress off you, Viper. I happen to like that baby on you."

"Yes, Don Matteo." I bat my eyelashes at him as I unzip the dress and let it fall to the floor.

"Come here." He kisses me roughly. "If I didn't want to fill your hole so badly, I'd shove it in that disobedient mouth and see how well you listen to your boss."

"There's always tomorrow," I remarked as if I wasn't completely turned on to the point that I'm going to come if he touches me like he did earlier. He lifts me up and carries me to the bed with his huge cock nudging my entrance as he falls onto the mattress. "Take me now, please. I want to be yours."

"You've always been mine, but it's nice to see the dangerous viper begging," he says with a smirk.

I can't let him get away with that smugness. "Don't push your luck, or you'll be begging later."

"I don't mind pleading between your thighs." Oh goodness, the man doesn't even care about my sass as long as I'm naked. He gives my panties a nice tug, and the lace just gives way. The bulbous head of his thick length rubs against my pussy, and I swear I can almost feel my orgasm on the surface.

"Don't tease me anymore. You know I'm crazy," I tell him, arching my hips to meet the fat tip.

"You ready for me?" I nod and he takes his dick in his hand, running it up and down between my folds and getting it all sopping wet from my horny hole. Staring me deep in the eyes, he pushes his way inside and says, "I love you, Vivian, and now you're mine for good."

He steals my breath, but it's not from the pain. That I can handle; it's from his words. Tears fill my eyes, and I wrap my arms around his neck, pulling his face down to mine, kissing my man. He growls and pulls out and pushes back in while deepening the kiss. Our words are garbled between kisses.

"Mine," he grunts through his long, deep strokes.

"Yes."

"Oh, fuck. I'm…" We're both on edge about to explode in a sweaty mess. Never had my fingers been this good to me.

"Matteo. Fuck. Yes. Please. Breed me." His hand wraps around my thigh, lifting it over his good shoulder and he ruts into me, fucking me slow and deep.

"You were made for me. So fucking tight," he says. Leaning down with his hands bracketing my head, he kisses me. His hips don't stop their assault on my tiny cunt, working it as we destroy the last of the boundaries between us. Sweat helps our bodies as we move perfectly together, made for each other. I cry out and come, clenching my walls around his massive girth that's beating down my womb.

"That's right, surrender to me, Viper. Give it to me. Show me who you belong to, amore." He pumps faster, roaring his orgasm a few moments later, sending his seed deep into me.

His hands are on me, and then I feel his lips kissing the scar on my shoulder. "I love this. I've dreamed of kissing it for so long, Vivian."

"What?" My heart nearly bursts at that revelation.

"That day, you told me it wasn't for me to see, but you had no idea that I'd already decided I'd kill another motherfucker if they tried to take you away from me." He brushes his fingers over the scar and then kisses it once more.

"You might be dangerous, but I'm obsessed."

I let out a light yawn. "Rest. I need to figure out what's going on." He kisses my head and sits up. Then, he pulls out his phone and makes some calls, but I'm too tired to pay any attention. Today has been too much. My mind and body have been through the wringer, and I need to get myself together.

CHAPTER EIGHT

MATTEO

AFTER VIVIAN FALLS ASLEEP, MY MEN HAVE clothes brought from the house for me and my mother delivers them upstairs so that no one comes to Vivian's room. She leaves them at the door and then gives me a big hug.

"I'm so glad you're safe," she sobs. My mother doesn't usually cry, but I guess today has been a lot for her. She's tough, and I suppose years of this shit has left her one strong woman.

"It's fine, Mom. It was only a flesh wound." I brush the tears away from her face.

She shakes her head. "I saw the footage on the security camera."

"What?"

"There are cameras in the bunker. One of them watches that exit." Damn, her parents keep track of her more than she or I thought.

"I'm sorry, Mom." Damn, that had to be torture. I couldn't imagine looking at my child being gunned down.

"I'm getting a wonderful daughter-in-law. You need her."

"I do, in every way." She hugs me once more, wiping her tears again before heading back downstairs.

I summon Vivian's brother to stand guard by the door because he's the only one I trust right now to look after my woman while we deal with this shit. "Hey, Gio, watch your sister with your life. I know you want to be down with everything, but given everything that's happened, there's no one I trust right now more than you for this. Even if no one else wants her dead, half these motherfuckers want to sleep with her."

"Damn, I hope I don't ever become that paranoid." He's not talking about the shooting. He's talking about men fighting over his sister. My sisters are beautiful and I'm sure that there will be boys flirting and I'll have to bust some heads later, but they're still pretty young.

"After tonight, you should understand why I'm this fucking nuts."

"I suppose so. Let's just say I hope I never have a reason to lose my shit like you do." Gio doesn't like to be bothered, and for his sake, I hope he finds someone who bothers the hell out of him because life isn't worth living until you find someone who gives you that excitement.

"Thanks."

"No problem. Anything for my little sister." We shake hands, and he pulls me in for a brotherly hug. He's been one of my many brains in the family. Unlike the others, he's not a fighter. Getting his hands dirty isn't something he likes, but when he has to get down, he's like his dad. Quiet and dangerous.

I head downstairs and find my parents sitting around with several other family heads including Enrico and June along with Dom Bianchi, his wife, and son.

"We need to get this handled."

"Understood."

"Where's Vivian?" her father asks, glaring at me. What can I say? What happened today would have happened tomorrow, so it's not that fucking big of a deal. He knew it was an eventuality the second I got her alone. For all he knew I banged his baby girl earlier.

"Sleeping."

A peace seems to come over him. "Good. This wasn't how her birthday was supposed to be."

"No, but remember, this was how our wedding ended, being Dom?" Mrs. Bianchi says.

He gives her a half smile. It probably means something to them, but this can't be celebrated. "Yes, amore. I do remember. It's been many years, my queen, but yes. We managed to rise out of the ashes and destroy everyone in our path, but tonight is different."

"How so?" I ask.

"Our family was here tonight, and they knew it. This wasn't just a strike on the Contis; this was a strike on all of us. They thought they could kill several birds with one big-ass bomb. If it wasn't for that sneaky-ass future wife of yours, we wouldn't have been any the wiser." Dom had a point that they were also targeted, so this was their fight as well.

"What does Vivian have to do with this?"

"When you went looking for her, I went around to check her usual escape routes. That's when we caught them in the act of sneaking in," Enrico says.

"If you hadn't gone to get her when you did..." June says.

"I don't want to even think about it." Dom's wife shakes her head and holds her husband's hand.

"We knocked out two dozen of their men tonight and destroyed their bombs, but that's not all they had, so we know we're not out of the woods just yet. We only had four injuries and two deaths from Neo's betrayal, thanks to the surprise we gave them. Not to mention Neo's death. That wife of yours is going to be an asset. It's a shame she's marrying you when I have other sons and nephews," Dom adds with a smile.

"You won't if they approach my bride," I snarl, standing up out of my chair.

Dom puts his hands up in surrender. "Good man. I understand what your wife means to you."

My father puts his hand on my good shoulder and I sit down. "Well, we can just toss Santos into this and claim they took him out," my father added.

"That could work should his family have questions, but I'm not worried about it."

"Vivian filled me in a little. She said our guy betrayed us because I didn't fall for his sister, which caused his wife to leave him. They said I was a pussy and would be easy to overthrow now that you handed over the Family to me. I don't know who his sister-in-law was, but the bitch is about to catch a knife from Vivian for sure."

"Do you remember the party we attended a few months back? There was a woman who kept flirting with you. You told her to back off and that you were spoken for and if she didn't, she'd find herself at the bottom of the Chicago River."

"Oh, yeah. Do you think that's her? Most women aren't stupid enough to approach me, so I guess that would make sense. Still, I don't remember her and couldn't point her out."

"That's because you didn't even notice her. She was beautiful and very put out," Marco says.

I shrug. "No one fucking matters but my viper, so I wouldn't have noticed."

"That's really fucking good," a hiss comes from behind me.

"Come sit down, little devil. You were supposed to be sleeping."

"I want heads to roll." She sits on my lap, wearing a tank top that only makes her look hot as hell, and a pair of sweats that hug her ass. She's got her blade in hand ready to gut a motherfucker, and that makes me hard as hell.

"Soon, but you're staying put and I'll bring you back a wedding present."

"What the hell?"

I swat her ass. "You will do what you're told. As the head of the family, I'm giving an order. Besides, you'll be here to guard the women and the house. Who the hell is better for that job than the queen?"

"You're lucky I'm in a compliant mood and I have witnesses."

"Doesn't he know it," my father says.

We go over our plan of attack, doing another sweep of every room in the house and checking the surveillance. Each family checks their residence to assure themselves that their homes were spared. Thankfully, we're in luck because we caught a couple of the vehicles fleeing the scene. Once we have our targets pinned down, we'll strike.

My beautifully enchanting woman's eyes get heavy, and I know it's time to call it a night. "We'll pick this up in the morning." What we need to do now is get married in the morning, but that will have to wait. We all part ways, and I take Vivian back to the mansion because from now on, she belongs in our bedroom and nowhere else. "Rest up,"

I tell my parents and give them a hug before heading up to my bedroom with my woman in my arms.

According to everyone, the wedding was considered called off, but we decided to have a small ceremony in the house with Father Anthony and our lawyer, who has the documents ready, so it will be as soon as possible.

In fact, I think we'll do that before shit gets crazy again.

We fall asleep until the early hours of the morning when I feel Vivian sliding over me, riding my lap. "Fuck, baby. If you're going to do that, please take him out and stuff him in that tight little cunt."

She pulls my cock free from my boxers and then mounts my length, sliding down it. "Oh Matteo, it feels so good."

I swat her ass and watch her tits jiggle. "So damn good, baby. Good morning." She rocks on me completely naked, taking my dick like she's been doing it her whole life until I fully wake up and take control. Flipping her onto her back, I rut into her hole, fucking that tiny hole, listening to each moan and scream, loving it. We both come, and I shoot loads of my nut into her depths like a fucking marksman.

"My queen. You drive me wild," I say, panting while kissing her. We both lie on the bed, and I'm exhausted.

"What time is it?" I grunt.

"I don't know. I woke up and you were moaning my name with your hand over your big cock, and I couldn't resist."

"My little devil." We kiss and pass out until the sun is completely up. Fuck, my shoulder aches, but I bite back the pain and remember that I have a lot to do.

Sliding out of bed, I hit the shower, protecting the bandage. I wish Vivian was in the shower with me, giving me a helping hand. Just as I'm about to get out, I see a sexy little thing entering the bathroom.

"Wow, what a sight." She stares right at my cock, making it harder than it was.

"Tell me about the sight. Keep licking those lips and you're going to help clean off my cock." She moves forward, pushing me back into the shower stall and then drops down to her knees completely naked and takes my thick length into her hand.

"It's so big, Matteo." She strokes it up and down from base to tip.

"Fuck," I groan, thighs shaking. I palm her head and slide my hand down to the base of her skull and slowly thrust my tip past her pretty lips.

"My little viper, keep going. Fuck. I'm going to come down that dirty mouth of yours." She moans around my meat, one hand going to her sex while the other pinches her nipples.

"That's it, baby, get off on sucking me down. Get that pussy nice and soaked because I'm going to stuff my big cock inside you."

"Please. I need it." She sucks me harder, but I can't take it anymore and I'm seconds from coming, so I pull her little sexy ass off me and lift her up.

"Vivian, that mouth of yours is dangerous." Spinning her to face the wall, I position myself at her entrance and slam into her hole, fucking her wet cunt. Our bodies press hard against one another, grinding and rocking while she spreads her hands out on the tiles. Fuck, her ring looks perfect, showing she belongs to me. Soon, there will be so much more proof that Vivian's only for me.

I lean in and bite down on her neck, growling like a fucking wild animal. "You're mine, Viper. Do you understand?"

"Yes, I'm yours, Matteo." Her breathy moans only spur me on.

"Fuck, I'm coming." I reach around and strum her pussy, and command her to come for me.

"Shit, I'm coming too." Her tight slit squeezes me, draining my balls dry.

"Fuck, I'm going to need another shower."

She turns her head and tilts it upward. "Well, that's good because I need one too, but at least we got that out of our system," she says with a giggle. Pulling out, I set her on her feet and turn the shower back on, letting the water get ready before moving us both under the giant spray.

It takes another twenty minutes for us to find our way out of the shower. We can't stop touching each other, but my woman is sore as fuck so I pump the brakes for now.

Wrapping her up in a fluffy white towel, I lead her to the bed while I go looking for something for her to wear. I should have packed her clothes, but she can wear some of my clothes until her mother or someone can bring her clothes over.

With my towel wrapped around my waist, I dig through and find her some boxers and a tee shirt that will float on her. "I'm going to call my mom and have her bring over clothes for me."

"That's a good idea."

"So what are you going to do?"

I check the time and see that we've woken up at the right time. "I have a meeting with the men in an hour, so slip on some of my clothes because I need to feed you, and then we can talk about getting married."

"Married? Don't you want to handle the Moreno Family first?"

"No. I want to marry you right away, and that means in a few hours, so when you talk to your mother, tell her to bring you the prettiest dress you have."

"You are crazy."

"You agreed."

"I did, but I don't mind waiting…unless you think…"

"I'm not worried about being killed. I want you to be my wife, and I want that now more than ever. Frankly, I'm pretty sure I made that clear before. Unfortunately, I had to wait for you to catch up with me. We might have grown up together, but I'm a few years older."

"The past couple of years have been hard for me, too. I didn't think we'd ever be anything more than family frenemies."

I pull her into my arms with my chin resting on the top of her head. "I'm sorry. Please don't cry. You're the toughest woman in the world, Vivian, and your tears are too much for me." I loosen my grip to stare into her eyes and then kiss her hard.

My phone rings. "Sorry, I have to get this."

"I know."

"Good morning, Mother."

"We made breakfast. Do you want us to bring it up to you, or will you join us down here?"

"We're coming down right now."

"Apparently, my mother has breakfast ready." I take her hand and we go down to see my parents, my siblings, her parents, and her siblings.

"Happy wedding day," our mothers say in unison.

"Thank you," Vivian says.

"Sit, Viper." I kiss her temple.

"You need to sit, son," my father says. "We have a big day. Enrico and I have been up for hours, and there are some things we need to discuss."

"Go on," I say, taking a sip of coffee.

"The Morenos called for a truce this morning."

Vivian barks out a laugh that turns into a snort.

"You heard the queen."

"Those are our thoughts as well. When they called and wanted to speak to me, I already thought it was an insult, but then to request it after what they pulled last night was even worse."

"Did you know that the whore who wanted your attention was a Moreno?"

"No."

"So they took it as an affront."

"Really, that's fucking pathetic. They'd die for that? I had a woman, so I had no interest in her? That's the stupidest shit I'd ever heard in my life."

"Word got out that Vivian was the girl at the warehouse that killed their enforcer."

"The one who almost took you out?"

"Yes, and that was her father. Apparently, it was a double insult."

"Listen, I don't want to go to war," Giovanni says.

"Then don't fight. We know how you feel about it," Enrico says.

"No, let me finish, Pops. I'm thinking we hit them financially. Cyberattack their finances and wipe them out from the inside out. Leave them with no fucking resources. They wouldn't know it was us. Remember—as far as they were aware, the Bianchi Family was here. Also, Landon Black's sons were supposed to be here, and you know Landon told Moreno to fuck off once."

"Yes, but we don't want to create problems for Black."

"I got a call from Landon Black Jr. this morning. His dad got word of the events and called, freaking out. He wants heads to roll as well." They are tight because Landon's a brilliant businessman like his father.

"Shit. Okay. So you think he'll help you?"

"He already started the process. He wants Moreno destroyed, and he's not above playing dirty where his family is concerned."

"Good. I say we attack from multiple fronts. I just don't want any casualties on our end."

"Gio, if this works out, you'll be getting a promotion." I wink at him. I could use him in my upper ranks. Right now, he handles the tech and finances, but that's it.

"I'm just trying to take care of my family." I sense a shift in Gio. I wonder if there's someone he met last night or this morning. Perhaps he's finally ready to enter the fold.

"Since we had this impromptu meeting, we can skip the one I had planned. So, everyone, let's enjoy our breakfast because we're getting married in two hours, and in the process, we'll dismantle their organizations."

"Sounds good."

"What's going on with Dom? Have any of you spoken to him or Luca?"

"Not yet. They arrived home safely, but we haven't discussed anything over open lines yet."

"I'll give them a call and apologize for yesterday's hiccup."

"Good, son. Let me know if you need anything else."

"You can sit in on the call with me." He nods, and we all finally get to enjoy this fantastic meal that our mothers prepared even though I have a chef.

CHAPTER NINE

VIVIAN

"You look amazing. Matteo's tongue is going to fall out of his mouth," Aunt June says, coming into the room. Thankfully she and Uncle Alessio were out of town when everything happened. We didn't need any more people to get hurt. They came back in a hurry when they got word. Yes, just like the Conti family, they aren't my real relatives, but I suppose they will be now.

"Thank you for coming here," I say. She pulls me in for a hug and squeezes tightly. She's Matteo's godmother and aunt, so they are all singing my praises again.

"Yes, well, we wouldn't let anyone hurt the family and stand by without doing anything. The wedding came as a surprise. Alessio thought he'd at least give you a week." They were in Italy, evaluating property for expansion of the Conti Family finances while enjoying some nice rest and relaxation.

I pulled away from her with my mouth open wide. "Wait —you knew he was going to ask me?"

"Ask? That boy has been obsessed with you for so long. Hence the reason we stayed away for your birthday. The less people in the way, the less people to interrupt his pursuit." I shake my head and smile.

"How did I miss it?" I questioned aloud.

"Because you weren't looking for it. You wanted to fight him, and he didn't want to show the world, making you a bigger target. Besides, if you knew he was tracking your every move, that would have given you more reason to try to sneak out of it," she confesses.

"Tracking my every move?" I step back, pressing my backside to the vanity, trying to put everything she said together. Was he tracking me? Was he that obsessed?

She turns pale and then covers her mouth. "I can't believe I let that slip."

"I need a moment alone," I say quietly, trying to hide my emotions.

She gives me a weak, apologetic smile. "Sure, sweetheart."

I'm standing in my beautiful wedding gown, looking in the mirror, thinking about what she said. He has been watching me for a long time. How long? When I accused him of putting a tracker in the ring, he said, "I don't need it." That's because he'd had me locked in his sights in other ways.

How does that make me feel? Most women would be pissed, scared, ready to run, but honestly, I feel loved. That man knows I'm fucking crazy and had me followed to keep me safe, always protecting me. Matteo has always been my protector before we had feelings for each other.

The door flies open, and I find a frantic Matteo staring at me with nervous eyes. "Vivian, I can explain."

I try to cover myself with a nearby robe, but it's too late. He's seen the dress. "You're not supposed to be in here. It's bad luck."

He shakes his head and stalks toward me, looking unhinged and insanely sexy. "I don't care. You have to listen to me. I'm not letting you leave me. Not now, not ever, so we don't need luck because you will be marrying me even if you fucking hate me because there's no other option." He runs his hands through his hair, mussing it all up. "Fuck, I told you I was obsessed."

I brush my hands over his scruffy face, trying to calm the madman while I smile at him. "Matteo, calm down, crazy. I love you, too." He finally stood still, shocked. His reaction gives me all the courage to continue. "Stalk me all you want. In fact, I look forward to one day figuring out how to elude you so you can hunt me down."

He takes my hand and kisses the inside of my palm. "Not until after we're married. I need a little peace before I have to catch your ass doing something bad."

I roll my eyes. "Fine, that's fair."

He drags my body to his, hands caressing my back. "God, I love you, Viper."

"No blood on the outfits. We need photos," my father calls out from the other side of the door. His voice coming out harsher than I expect from him.

"He's afraid I'll stab you," I whisper. After almost losing him, I can't imagine causing him any more pain. Matteo is my everything and I live for him.

"I think he's just trying to stop me from fucking you," Matteo grumbles, rubbing his hard body up against mine, proving that even when he's worried about losing me, he's still ready to go. The sensual caress is more than enough to heat up my entire being and I want him right now.

"What a pity." I pout, rubbing my core against his big stick. "I could go for some frantic Matteo sex." My body is on fire thinking about what he can do to me with his tongue and his huge cock. For a virgin the man is gifted. Not that I had any experience before him, but he knows how to get me off. I'm putty in his hands.

He brushes his lips against mine, kissing me so gently until our arms and hands move up and down each other, groping body parts, moaning. "Later. I'm going to take you dirty and hard," he says huskily.

"Enough in there. We have a wedding to attend," my father says, pounding on the door again. We pull apart and I adjust my dress to keep everything tucked into place.

Matteo opens the door with a grumble. "You're lucky that you're Vivian's dad and like an uncle to me." My father doesn't even bother to flinch because he's always been a badass, but because their bond is tight.

"That's the only reason I let you get away with marrying my daughter so easily," he says, nudging Matteo out the door, but avoiding his injured arm. My future husband gives me one last glance, smiling at me with a look of pure adoration before he disappears down the stairs.

My father then turns to me, smiling. "You look beautiful and I'm happy that I get to give you away to someone who truly loves you. Come on, my devil princess."

"Thank you, daddy," I say, giving him a big hug.

He releases me and then takes my hand. "Let's get you downstairs before that man loses his mind." There are many fathers who would disapprove because we're so young, and yes, I'm eighteen, but I'm also a mafia princess with the head of the mafia completely obsessed with me, so it works.

The wedding is beautifully simple with our closest family around and some security. Father Anthony stands at the front waiting for me as my father takes me to Matteo, who is itching to make me his permanently.

We say our 'I dos' and are pronounced husband and wife. Now it's time for him to worship me. He leans in and pulls me close, claiming my mouth without hesitation. I melted into his arms, my hands sliding into his hair as I let out a moan. He cups my ass, lifting me against his length. A cough comes from the side. We break apart to find our fathers holding back a chuckle.

Blushing, I duck my head. Matteo lifts my chin and shakes his head. "I'll kiss you anytime I want, my wife. I don't care who is watching."

"That was more than a kiss," Matteo's brother says.

"Congratulations to the newly wedded Mr. and Mrs. Matteo Conti," Father Anthony says. Everyone cheers, congratulating us.

We make it through the crowd, greeting and thanking everyone. The aisle is packed with all our family members, and I make sure to hug my mother who has tears in her eyes. "I love you, mom. Thank you for teaching me what real love is."

"Baby girl, you are our heart and soul. Remember, even when he's a pain in the ass that you can always return the favor." She winks and steps away to give others a chance to speak with me.

My sisters-in-law are gushing over my dress but scolding their brother about the rushed wedding. They are sweet girls; Chiara's sixteen and Giulia's fourteen and ready to meet their future husbands. "When we get married, he better not rush it, or it ain't happening," Giulia says.

"How long do you need to plan a wedding?" Matteo asks.

"A year at least," Chiara answers.

Matteo holds my hand, squeezing it tight. "If he lets you plan it for a year out, he doesn't want to marry you, and he's not worth your time. Besides, what the hell do you need that takes that long? You're already planning everything now."

"You just don't understand," Chiara says, rolling her eyes.

"I understand that I couldn't wait for my woman. Still, you have a long time until you find the right one." We walk away from them because I'm not sure Dario or Matteo is willing to let them even date any time in the near future. We greet more of our family and friends as husband and wife, making our rounds before it's time for our toast.

As we celebrate with a glass of wine before our food, Matteo makes an announcement. "Yesterday we lost a couple of men, and I haven't forgotten. They will be laid to rest this week and their families compensated. However, after that, I'll be taking the next two weeks off, afterward as I take my bride on our honeymoon. We will be enjoying a sunny beach as the weather grows chilly here."

I leaned in and asked, "Are you serious?"

"Yes. You deserve a honeymoon, and besides, I have to make up for that shitty birthday."

"Hey, my birthday wasn't all bad, husband," I confess.

"Say that again," he growls, tightening his hold on my waist.

"Husband." I kiss him in front of the entire family who clap and cheer. He picks me up with his good arm and I cling to him. "Husband."

Matteo's phone rang just as the gate sensor went off. "Yes, okay. Send them in."

"It's the police." Two detectives come that we've dealt with over time. They don't want trouble with us, so they just ask a few questions and carry on. It's easier than getting in the way. The Conti Family owns many political officials. Chicago's more corrupt than it ever was under Capone, and we have a big chokehold on it. That's why the Morenos were so eager to come after us. Fools. Matteo would never give an inch. He's worse than his father.

"How can we help you, Detectives?" he asks, dressed in his sexy suit. I bite my bottom lip, staring at his naturally powerful presence.

"You're in the middle of a wedding," one dick remarks after taking in my dress.

He brings my hand to his mouth, and he kisses it. "Yes, I have just married the former Vivian Barone."

"Oh, well, congratulations. We didn't mean to interrupt. Given the events of yesterday, we hadn't expected a wedding. We're concerned about the retribution and the ongoing war that could come from this." I find it suspicious and I'm sure a lot of hackles were raised. I check around the room and all the men have stiffened up as if we're going to have a round two.

"Calm down, fellas. We have no intention of letting a squabble between some of our employees and Moreno's employees get in the way."

"Moreno says you have a hit on him," the detective says.

"Interesting...are you working for him?" I asked. After Philo's betrayal, it's not hard to suspect that some cops have taken sides.

"Heavens, no, but when we spoke to him to assess the situation per our chief's request, he gave us that information."

"Well, that's news to us. I have no intention of doing anything to anyone but my wife for the foreseeable future. The Morenos lie. It's their way of life and if I were you, I'd be careful because the more you dig in with them, the more likely you'll end up in their crosshairs." Matteo's warning is clear as they grow unsteady on their feet.

The lead detective steps a little closer with balls of brass. "And we don't have that problem with your family?"

"Do I have a reason to not like you? No. Well, then, Detectives, I suggest you relax and focus on other matters. The Morenos aren't worth your time. If you'll excuse us, we've already had enough interruptions." They nod and take their leave.

The second they're gone, Matteo looks at Gio and says, "Get their finances. They're working for the Morenos. I don't know who they think they're fooling, but they need to try harder."

"Could that have been more obvious?" I exclaimed, looking at the elder generation who are standing next to Matteo. "Either they are complete morons, or they're trying to see how much they can extract for the Morenos." I'd like to shoot them in the face because they almost took my husband away from me.

"Nothing. Well, let's continue with our celebration." He slides his hand around my waist and twirls me around the room as if there's music playing. Suddenly, the household surround sound comes on and music plays. "Our first dance, my wife."

"I'm obsessed." All the married couples start dancing around us.

"Good because that makes two of us, and as you can see, it's for life." He presses our hands on his heart where he's had me for years.

"It's perfect."

EPILOGUE

MATTEO

THE BEACH WAS BEAUTIFUL WITH MY QUEEN IN her many tiny swimsuits. Today is our last day on this island paradise. Of course we were isolated, and our security kept their distance so no one gets an accidental view of my wife. There is no way I'd tolerate men looking at her perversely. She's only for me and I make everyone aware of it.

We made special appearances in the beach town just in case the police needed to know our whereabouts. We let them believe that we were just a happily newly married couple, but we are so much more.

It's the strangest thing. Several heads of the Moreno family committed suicide in the past week. A call came in around nine to alert us that the Moreno heads had died, or at least most of them had. Although our relationship with our enemies briefly picked up thanks to Gio.

However, it worked out for the best. Some of the detectives believe the suicides were because they lost all their assets to Russian hackers who remain untraceable.

The last of the Moreno Family took their wives and kids and fled the state. It's amazing what happens when you lose almost everything. We're sure they have some hidden assets, but it won't be long until they cross the wrong men in Mexico. They had a tendency to upset the wrong people, especially people like the Bianchi Family who had been like us and planned their attack with skill.

It's amazing how easily someone's demise could look like suicide.

"Hey there, Don Matteo."

I spin around and find my bride staring at me in a sultry green dress that accents her hair and brings out the color of her eyes. "There's my viper."

"Like you didn't know where I was."

"No, says the woman who is always ready to strike. What's going on in those dangerous eyes and vicious mind?"

"Nothing." She's hiding something from me and I don't like it. It's too soon for her take a pregnancy test or maybe it isn't with the new technology, but I don't believe that's the bullshit lie that fell off her tongue.

"You know how I feel about your lies."

"Yes, but we're going to be late for dinner."

"They'll hold our seats." She bites on the side of her bottom lip, and I sense she's upset by something. "What's going on, wife?"

"There was a woman on the beach, watching us today." She looks out toward the beach as if the bitch is still there.

"What do you mean? Why didn't you say anything?"

"I didn't realize it at first, but then I caught a glimpse and sent the drone up."

"You should have said something," I snarl.

"I didn't want to let on that we knew, just in case she got away."

"Okay, so was she just curious that I was fucking breeding my wife?" I asked, hoping she wasn't upset with me.

"No, she's the one who was obsessed. I contacted Black, and she came up in several videos and photos where you were at." Damn, my woman was on a mission while I took some important calls, and I thought she was spending all that time napping and bathing. She handed me her phone to view the picture. It's the event I was at. I'd been focused on the appetizers and ignoring the woman. She shows me a close-up of the woman and then zooms out. She was staring right at me. Fuck—this woman wasn't just interested, she was a stalker.

"Damn it. I'll deal with this." I handed her phone back before I crushed the fucker with my anger.

"No, you won't. I don't want this bitch near you. You're mine, or have you forgotten?" God, her jealous possessiveness is sexy as fuck, but I have to protect her at all costs and of course she has nothing to worry about since she's had me since day one.

"Don't even start that, woman." I pull her in for a kiss just as a shot comes off, hitting the veranda we're staying at.

I rushed her into the house for safety. Three more shots are fired, but our men are on it and a cry can be heard before a giant splash into the ocean. "That's it. This bitch is sleeping with the fishes tonight." I'd say she watches too many movies, but we're on what's supposed to be an isolated beach.

"Find her and make sure the shooter's dead," I shout out, pinning my wife down before she does something dumb like run into the crossfire.

"Wow, I thought I was crazy for you," she says, clinging to me behind a large sofa.

"You are, but I guess there are levels of crazy. And I think I tap out at anything above your batshit level." No woman could ever compare to my Vivian. Even if she was a sweet, meek little wife, I probably be just as nuts about her. Hell, I hope she does calm down when we have our babies. She doesn't need to take any unnecessary risks.

"Good, because you're mine."

Several rounds of footsteps make their way to us. "Boss, Marco and Justin have her. She's still breathing, but just barely."

I stand and help my wife up, checking to see if she has any scrapes. With her looking as pristine as usual, I address my men. "Good—bring her in. We have questions before we take care of business. Make sure we don't have any witnesses." They leave to deal with the matter.

"We need to figure out how she got on this island and how she knew where we'd be," Vivian says.

"Tell me about it."

"Well, it wasn't a state secret where we were going, but since she's obsessed, I'm guessing she's going hardcore and following us." Most wouldn't notice it because the Morenos never let their women get involved, so if anyone saw this chick, they would have dismissed it. I'm guessing she changed her disguises so they wouldn't recognize her.

"Is she dead?" the bitch says as she's being dragged in by Vivian's older brother Marco. "I hope she's dead. Ouch. Don't hurt me. My Matty wouldn't like it."

"Your Matty?" Vivian whispers to me. I don't know this fucking woman. When she comes into the room and sees us, she screams, "You bitch. You are still alive. Why didn't you die?"

"You need better aim. Who the hell are you, and why are you after my man?" Viper bites out.

"He's mine."

"No, I don't know you," I say honestly.

"You're lying, Matty. We spoke for hours when we created that ring. It was for me, and yet you gave it to her."

"Holy fuck." Everything is starting to make sense. I remember the call, but then my wife is beside me, fuming with rage.

"Oh, so suddenly you remember her," Vivian snaps, getting out of line. I grab my wife by the waist and drag her to my side, cupping her chin.

"Wife, you better quit your shit because the second this is over, I'm going to punish you for doubting my fidelity." I mean that with my whole damn chest and I need my bride to understand it's always and only her.

"You know that shit doesn't work on me," she hisses, giving me that attitude I'm going to fuck out of her...at least for a while.

"She doesn't deserve you," the tied up broad says.

"Bitch, shut up," my viper hisses at her and then turns her ire back at me. "So is she telling the truth? Do you know her?"

"Yes and no. I ordered the ring custom made, and the specifications were done through a service for specialty clients. I only spoke to her on the phone once about the sizing and design shape. How I wanted it to look like a snake's eye, but I didn't remember her name or anything. In fact, all other conversations were done with the owner, a man, but he had to step out and asked her to handle the specs. That's all. Shit, I ordered the ring two years ago."

A smile spreads over Vivian's face as the truth hits her, and then a realization does as well, changing her expression. The same one that hit me too. "Oh my goodness. That's why she was able to track us. The ring."

My head shakes as I realize my error. "That's why she was able to be at events I was at. I carried it with me everywhere I went. A piece of you with me so it was like you were there."

"Fucking hell, I love you, Matteo." She kisses me in front of the crazy woman, which sets her off. She tries lunging out of her chair, but Vivian kicks her in the throat with sexy heels.

"Fuck, you crushed her hyoid bone," Marco says.

"Good. Now she'll shut the fuck up. Clean up this mess. I'm on my honeymoon, and I'm still dealing with trouble."

"You'll always be trouble, my devil queen." I chuckle and so does her brother. She glares at him and then stares at me with that audacity I love.

"You love it."

"I love you," I say, kissing her roughly.

EPILOGUE

VIVIAN

"I'm not ready for babies. Oh my goodness," I whisper to myself.

I hold this little one in my arms, and it hits me with all the feelings involved. My love for this little person makes me want to kick my own ass for being such a bad kid. My parents put up with so much shit because they loved me, and I gave my dad in particular pure hell. Always sneaking around, trying to follow him, almost getting myself killed.

"Matteo, we made this little boy," I say, tears sliding down my cheeks. He leans in and wipes them away with the pads of his thumbs. His touch alone makes me feel secure.

"Yes, we did," he says, sliding onto the bed beside me. He cradles his arm around my shoulder, kissing the scar, and then bends to kiss the top of our son's head. "Hello, my son. I love you." I nestle my body against my darling husband and let him support our weight.

"Our parents will be here soon," I say.

"I know. They're excited to see the first addition to the family, but you need to rest, my little momma."

He kisses my lips so tenderly that I can't help but confess my fears. "I'm scared, Matteo."

"Why?" he asks, rubbing my arm while staring into my eyes.

"I'm not a good mom like my mother or yours."

He chuckles softly and lightly sighs. Cupping my chin, he says, "You're the viper. You're going to be a great mother. You're strong enough to protect our kids, smart enough to teach them, loving enough to worry about them going into danger, and you're sneaky enough to catch them before they do some crazy shit."

A bubbling little coo comes from our son and we both laugh. "Sorry, little man. I'll try to watch my mouth." He rubs our son's fuzzy little head. He's like both of us and he was born with a full head of dark, almost black hair. We rest for a few minutes in the silent peace as he closes his eyes and sleeps.

"Knock, knock," my mother says, sticking her head in the hospital room. She comes in with a bunch of balloons, followed by Matteo's mother and our dads. I'm sure our brothers will be here soon along with Aunt June and Uncle Alessio.

There is no doubt that we'll be leaving by tomorrow, but no one can wait for the babies to be here. Matteo's brother has been in Italy for the past year, so we have hardly seen him. He came after the attack on us, but then had to get back to his business. He'll be here soon to meet his nephew as well.

"There's our grandbaby." Matteo stands up to give me space. I hand him the baby so they can see him while I rest.

"Look, Dario," May sobs. "He's so cute. Oh my goodness." She lightly caresses his downy cheek.

They gush over the little guy for a bit while my dad comes up and hugs me. "How are you, my devil princess?" he asks, kissing the top of my head.

"I wanted to say I'm sorry, Dad."

He takes a seat on the edge of my bed and asks, "What? Why?"

"For giving you guys so much shit. Seeing our son, I know how I'd do anything to keep him safe and all you two had to go through with me."

He laughs heartily while taking my hand in his. "Hey, I expected more of you to be devils. The fact that it was mostly you is not so bad. I needed one of you to be a bit more like me. Marco is definitely giving it his best, but you came out swinging, kiddo." He hugged me tight, and I remember that he always spurred me on a bit when Mom wasn't looking.

"I love you, Dad."

"I love you, my little devil princess." He kisses the top of my head, and I know things are going to be just fine.

EPILOGUE

MATTEO

SHE'S FUCKING SLICK. STILL, I SMILED TO MYSELF as I hunt her down. It's been a while since she's played this game, but I love it when she does, honing both our skills as she undoes all her tracking devices and limits all her uses, demanding I find her with other clues.

She understands my level of crazy matches hers to the point that I'd almost chip her ass, but then these little games wouldn't be any fun. I love hunting my prey, but my patience grows thin with every second that passes, and I don't have her in my arms.

Being obsessed with my wife is one thing that hasn't changed in the decade that we've been married. Ten years and I'm so damn addicted to her that my heart is tied to hers.

I listen to the sounds of the trees, hearing nothing in the night air except for the cicadas and then there's that tiny little crack, letting me know that she's nearby. It took two hours for me to figure out that she wasn't where she said she'd be; that's because I trusted my bride to behave on our anniversary, but no, someone wants her fucking spanking.

"Come out now, Viper. If I come get you, no orgasms, baby," I warn her. It's bullshit because hearing her scream my name while I'm buried deep in her with my dick, tongue or fingers is a must. Other than when she gave birth to our babies and the weeks after, I always make it a priority to wring out at least one orgasm out of her.

"That's not fair." She pouts, coming out of the darkness in an all dark-green skintight jumpsuit that has a scale pattern on it. She's trying to get knocked up again so that everyone understands she's more than taken, she's possessed by the Don.

"Fucking hell, you left the house in that?" My mouth nearly falls to the floor when I see how her ample breasts are hugged by the material that zips just halfway up her cleavage, leaving so much exposed. She looks like a sexy vixen that's about to destroy Batman.

"You like it?" she asks as if there is any other answer than hell yes.

I tilt my chin up and down because I can't trust myself to speak just yet. I clear my throat and snarl my feelings. "Just for my eyes only."

"Then come this way, Don Matteo. I have something special for you." She takes my hand and leads me to a small cabin where she must have been hiding. Inside, there's a table set up with chilled wine, and a bed made for lovers. I wonder who the hell helped her with this.

"Happy Anniversary," she blurts out full of pride for her setup.

An overwhelming feeling of jealousy takes over my common sense. Everything is set too intimately, and I'd hate to have anyone think of trying to replace me. "I hoped none of the guys helped with this."

She gives me a slow eye roll. "Of course not. I wouldn't trust anyone here with me except my besties." So all her sisters-in-law and cousins teamed up to make this happen.

I turn to stare at the love of my life and know she's fucking way sneakier than I give her credit for. "So about that punishment?" She tugs at my belt.

"One moment, beautiful." I make a call and ensure that the kids are watched for the entire weekend because my wife isn't going to be walking or sitting well for a while once we're done celebrating.

As soon as my call is over, I take a seat on the bed, and pat my thighs. "Let's start on my lap, baby. Then we'll go from there." She jumps into my arms and I can't stop myself from letting her know how much I adore her. "God, I love you, Vivian Conti." I crushed her lips to mine until she's mush in my grasp. Then I toss her over my knees to let the fun begin.

THE END

ABOUT THE AUTHOR

Find me on:

Website/Newsletter: www.cmsteele.com

Amazon Author Page: www.amazon.com/C-M-Steele/e/
B00MQ9FPZS/

Facebook: www.facebook.com/CMsteele2014

Instagram: https://www.instagram.com/c.m._steele/

Twitter: https://twitter.com/Author_CMSteele

Bookbub: https://www.bookbub.com/authors/c-m-steele

ALSO BY C.M. STEELE

A Best Friends Duet:

Picture Perfect * Instant Obsession

Best Friends Series:

Always You * His Dirty Secret * Sleep Tight

Bianchi Crime Family:

Married to the Mob * Captured by the Mob * Owned by the Mob

Cavanaugh Security Series:

Protecting Macy * Securing Blake

The Cline Brothers of Colorado:

Whatever it Takes * Taking Whatever He Wants * Finding Paradise

The Conti Crime Family Series:

Alessio * Dario * Enrico * Matteo * Gio

Dirty Boss Series:

My Pet * My Cookie * My Flower * My Valentine

(Now on Audio)

The Falling Hard & Fast Series:

Falling for the Boss * Falling for the Enemy * Falling Hard

The Fiore Family:

Christmas with the Beast * Christmas with the Boss * Christmas with the Sheriff

Gimme Series:

Sugar * Luck * Rain * Cream * Heat * Love

My Miracle * Nailing my Wife

Say Something Series:

Say Uncle * Say Please * Say Uncle: Doggy Style

Second Generation:

Say Yes

Seasons of Love:

Wet Summer * Autumn Falls * Winter Frost

Sister Switch:

Testing Her Professor * Assisting Her Boss

A Steele Christmas:

Mason's Winter * Perfectly Wrapped * The Company You Keep

A Steele Fairy Tale:

My Gold * My Forever * My Property * My Prince Charming

A Steele Riders Family Novella Series:

Sammie * Roxie * Mike * Dylan

Steele Riders MC Series:

Boomer * Mick * Jackson * Doc * Beast * Ghost

Wrench * Blade * Boss * Cowboy * Law *Cyber

Steele Riders MC 2nd Generation Series:

Will * Julian

Southern Hospitality:

Down South * Gone South

Sweet Temptation Bay:

A Taste Of Honey * The Mayor's Surrender * Trapped with my Stalker

Sweetheart's Treats:

Sweet Surprise * Doctor's Orders, Sweetheart * Sweet Surrender

Twin Sin:

Stalk Me Please * Sinful Intent

White Wolf Ridge Series:

Turner

Wolfe Creek Series:

Wolfe's Den * Beta: Her Alpha

Raging Kane * Written in History

Standalones:

Auctioned to the Kingpin* Buying Love * Conquering Alexandria

Ecstasy Captured * Grant's Deal * In Heat * Intense

Killer Abs * Love Discovered * Loving My Neighbor * Lucky Ride

Mrs. Valentine * My Christmas Gift

Rainy Days * Stormy Nights * Red Hot Nights

Room Service * Scarred * Sharp Curves

So Wrong * Standing There

The Mobster's Virgin * The Wedding Guest